THE SICILIAN BANDIT

by

Alexandre Dumas

British Library Cataloguing-in-Publication Data
A catalogue record for this book is available from the
British Library

Contents

Alexandre Dumas   5

CHAPTER I.—Introduction—Palermo.   7

CHAPTER II.—Bruno And Ali.   25

CHAPTER III.—The Fatal Bridal.   35

CHAPTER IV.—The Prince And The Bandit.   43

CHAPTER IV.—The Robber's Castle.   54

CHAPTER VI.—A Bandit's Gratitude.   66

CHAPTER VII.—A Brigand's Vengeance.   78

CHAPTER VIII.—-Treachery.   87

CHAPTER IX.—The Siege.   97

CHAPTER X.—The Chapelle Ardente.   110

CHAPTER XI.—Death Of The Bandit.   118

CHAPTER XII.—Conclusion.   126

Alexandre Dumas

Alexandre Dumas was born in Villers-Cotterêts, France in 1802. His parents were poor, but their heritage and good reputation – Alexandre's father had been a general in Napoleon's army – provided Alexandre with opportunities for good employment. In 1822, Dumas moved to Paris to work for future king Louis Philippe I in the Palais Royal. It was here that he began to write for magazines and the theatre.

In 1829 and 1830 respectively, Dumas produced the plays Henry III and His Court and Christine, both of which met with critical acclaim and financial success. As a result, he was able to commit himself full-time to writing. Despite the turbulent economic times which followed the Revolution of 1830, Dumas turned out to have something of an entrepreneurial streak, and did well for himself in this decade. He founded a production studio that turned out hundreds of stories under his creative direction, and began to produce serialised novels for newspapers which were widely read by the French public. It was over the next two decades, as a now famous and much loved author of romantic and adventuring sagas, that Dumas produced his best-known works – the D'Artagnan romances, including The Three Musketeers, in 1844, and The Count of Monte Cristo, in 1846.

Dumas made a lot of money from his writing, but he was almost constantly penniless as a result of his extravagant lifestyle and love of women. In 1851 he fled his creditors to Belgium, and then Russia, and then Italy, not returning to Paris until 1864. Dumas died in Puys, France, in 1870, at the age of 68. He is now enshrined in the Panthéon of Paris alongside fellow authors Victor Hugo and Emile Zola. Since his death, his fiction has been translated into almost a hundred languages, and has formed the basis for more than 200 motion pictures.

CHAPTER I.—INTRODUCTION—PALERMO.

It is with cities as with men—chance presides over their foundation; and the topographical situation of the first, and the social position of the latter, exercise a beneficial or an evil influence over their entire existence.

There are noble cities which, in their selfish pride of place, have refused to permit the erection even of a few humble cottages on the mountain on which their foundations rested: their domination must be exclusive and supreme; consequently they have remained as poor as they are proud.

There are villages so humble as to have taken refuge in the recesses of the valley—have built their farmsteads, mills, and cottages on the margin of a brook, and, protected by the hills that sheltered them from heat and cold, have passed an almost unknown and tranquil life, like that of men without ardour and without ambition—terrified by every sound, dazzled by every blaze of light, and whose whole happiness consists in shade and silence.

There are, again, others that have commenced their existence as paltry hamlets on the sea-shore, and which, by degrees, have seen sailing vessels succeed the simple boat, and noble ships the tiny barque—whose modest huts have given place to lordly palaces, while the gold of Potosi and the wealth of the Indies flow into their ample ports.

It is for these reasons that we give to cold, inanimate nature epithets that truly belong to man's nobility alone. Thus we say, Messina the noble, Syracuse the faithful, Girgenti the magnificent, Trapani the invincible, and Palermo the blessed.

If ever there was a city predestined to be blessed—that city is Palermo. Situated beneath a cloudless sky, on a luxuriously fertile plain, and sheltered by a belt of mountains, in the centre of a picturesquely beautiful country, its ample ports open to receive the gentle flow of the azure sea.

There is nothing more beautiful than the days at Palermo, except it be the nights—those eastern nights, so clear and balmy, in which the murmur of the sea, the rustling of the breeze, and the busy hum of the town seem like a universal concert of love, during which all created things, from the wave to the tree, from the tree to man himself, breathe a mysterious sigh.

At times, however, the sea suddenly assumes a livid tint; the wind drops, the noise of the city is hushed; a few bloodied clouds travel rapidly from the south to the north; these clouds foretell the coming of the dread sirocco, that scorching blast, borne in the sands of Libya and carried to Europe by the southerly gales: immediately everything animate droops and becomes oppressed and suffering, and the whole island feels as when Etna threatens. Animals and men alike seek shelter, and when they have found it, they crouch in breathless fear, for the blast has taken away all courage, paralysed the strength, and deadened every faculty; and this lasts until a purer air from the Calabrian hills restores the strength and appears to renew their existence, and on the morrow all again is pleasure and mirth.

It was the evening of the month of September, 1803, when the sirocoo had lasted throughout the entire day; but at sunset the sky became clear, the sea resumed its azure tint, and a few blasts of cool air blew over the Liparian Archipelago. This atmospheric change had such an influence on all animated beings, that they gradually revived from their state of torpor, and you might have imagined you were present at a second creation, the more so from the fact of Palermo being, as we have already said, a perfect garden of Eden.

Among all the daughters of Eve who, in the paradise they inhabit, make love their principal occupation, there was one who will play a very important part in the course of this history. That we may direct the attention of our readers to her, and to the place in which she dwelt, let them leave Palermo by the San-Georgio gate along with us, leaving the castle of St Mark on the right, and, reaching the Mole, they will follow the course of the sea-shore for some distance, and stop before the delightful villa of the Prince of Carini, the Viceroy of Sicily under Ferdinand the Fourth, who had just returned from Naples to take up his abode in it.

On the first floor of this elegant villa, in a chamber tapestried with azure-blue silk, the ceiling of which was ornamented with fresco painting, a female, simply attired in a snow-white morning dress, was reclining on a sofa, her arms hung listlessly, her head was thrown back, and her hair dishevelled; for an instant she might have been taken for a marble statue, but a gentle tremor ran through her frame, colour gradually came to her cheeks, her eyes began to open, the beautiful statue became animated, sighed, stretched out its hand to a little silver bell placed on a table of peliminta marble, rang it lazily, and, as if fatigued with the effort she had made, fell back again on the sofa.

The silvery sound, however, had been heard, the door opened, and a young and pretty waiting-maid, whose disordered toilet declared that she, as well as her mistress, had felt the influence of the African wind, appeared on the threshold.

"Is it you, Teresa?" said her mistress, languidly, and turning her head. "It is enough to kill one: is the sirocco still blowing?"

"No, signora, it has quite passed over, and we begin to breathe again."

"Bring me some iced fruit, and let me have a little air."

Teresa obeyed these orders with as much promptitude as the remains of her languor would allow; she placed the refreshments on the table, and opened the window that looked out on the sea.

"Look, madame la comtesse," she said, "we shall have a magnificent day to-morrow; and the air is so clear that you can plainly see the island of Alicari, although the day is drawing to a close."

"Yes, yes, the air is refreshing; give me your arm, Teresa; I will try if I can drag myself as far as the window."

The attendant approached her mistress, who replaced on the table the refreshment her lips had scarcely touched, and, resting on Teresa's shoulder, walked languidly towards the balcony.

"How this delightful breeze revives one," she observed, as she inhaled the evening air; "bring me my chair, and open the other window that looks into the garden,—that will do. Has the prince returned from Montreal?"

"Not yet, my lady," replied Teresa.

"So much the better; I would not have him see me in this wretched state, so pale and weak: I must look dreadfully."

"Madame la comtesse never looked more beautiful than at this moment, and I am certain that in the whole city we see from this window, there is not a woman who would not be jealous of your ladyship."

"Do you include the Marchioness of Rudini and the Princess of Butera?"

"I except no one," replied the attendant.

"Ah, I see the prince has been bribing you to flatter me, Teresa."

"I assure you, madame, I only tell you what I think."

"Oh, what a delightful place Palermo is!" said the countess, taking a deep inspiration.

"Especially when one is two-and-twenty years of age, and rich and beautiful," continued Teresa, smiling.

"You have but completed my thoughts, and on that account I wish to see every one about me cheerful and happy. When is your marriage to take place, Teresa?" Teresa made no answer. "Is not Sunday the day fixed upon?" continued the countess.

"Yes, signora," answered her attendant with a sigh.

"Why do you sigh? Have you not made up your mind?"

"Oh, yes, certainly."

"Have you any dislike to the marriage!"

"No; I believe Gaetano is a good lad, and that he will make me happy. Besides, this marriage will enable me to remain with madame la comtesse, and that is my most earnest wish."

"Then why did you sigh?"

"Pray pardon me, my lady, but I was thinking of our native country."

"Our native country!" echoed the countess.

"Yes; madame la comtesse may remember, while at Palermo, that she had left a foster sister at the village of which her father was the signor; and when she wrote for me to come to her, I was about to be married to a young man belonging to Bauso."

"Why did you not tell me of that? The prince, at my recommendation, would have taken him into his service."

"Oh, he would not become a servant," said Teresa; "he was too proud for that."

"Indeed!" said the countess.

"Yes; he had before then refused the situation of shepherd to the Prince of Goto."

"He was a gentleman, then, this young man?"

"No, madame la comtesse; he was but a simple mountaineer," said Teresa, in a melancholy tone.

"What was his name?"

"Oh, I do not think that your ladyship would recollect it,"

said Teresa, eagerly.

"And do you then regret his loss?"

"I cannot tell; I only know that if I were to become his wife instead of Gaetano's, I should be obliged to work for my living; and that would be a laborious task for me, after leading so easy and pleasant a life under madame la comtesse."

"And yet, Teresa, is it not true that people accuse me of pride and violence?" asked the countess.

"Madame is very good to me, that is all I can say," replied Teresa.

"The nobles of Palermo say so, because the Counts of Castel Nuovo were ennobled by Charles the Fifth, while the Ventimillas and the Partanas descend, as they pretend, from Tancred and Rogero: but that is not the reason the women hate me; they conceal their hatred under the cloak of disdain, and they neglect me because Rodolpho loves me, and they are jealous of the viceroy's love; they do all they can to seduce him from me; but they will never succeed, for my beauty is greater than theirs—Carini tells me so every day, and so do you, story-teller."

"You have here a greater flatterer than either his excellency or myself," said Teresa, archly.

"Who is that?" asked the countess.

"The countess's mirror."

"Foolish girl!" said the countess, with a gratified smile. "There, go and light the tapers of the Psyche." The attendant obeyed her mistress's orders. "Now shut that window, and leave me; there will be sufficient air from the garden."

Teresa obeyed, and left the room. Scarcely did the countess perceive that she was gone, than she seated herself before the Psyche, and smiled as she looked at and admired herself in the glass.

A wonderful creature was the Countess Emma, or rather Gemma, for, from her very infancy, her parents had added a G to her baptismal name; and, on account of this addition, she called herself Diamond. She was certainly wrong in confining her origin to the signature of Charles the Fifth, for in her slight and pliant form, you might recognise an Ionian origin; in her black and expressive eyes, a descendant of the Arabs; and in her fair and vermilion skin, a daughter of Gaul. She could equally boast of her descent from an Athenian archon, a Saracen emir, and a Norman chieftain; she was one of those beauties that in the first instance were found in Sicily alone, at a later time in one town alone in the world— Arles. So that, instead, of calling the artifices of the toilet to her assistance, as she intended in the first instance, Gemma found herself more charming in her partial dishabille.

The glass, being placed before the window that was left open, reflected the sky from its surface, and Gemma, without intention or thought, wrapt herself up in a vague and delicious pleasure, counting in the glass the images of the stars as they each appeared in their turn, and giving them names as they successively appeared in the heavens.

Suddenly it appeared as if a rising shadow placed itself before the stars, and that a face appeared behind her; she turned herself quickly round and beheld a man standing at the window. Gemma rose and opened her mouth with the intention of screaming for assistance, when the stranger, springing into the chamber, clasped his hands, and said in supplicating accents—

"In the name of heaven do not call out, madame! for on my honour, you have nothing to fear: I will do you no harm."

Gemma fell back into her chair, and the apparition and words of the stranger were succeeded by a moment's silence, during which she had time to cast a rapid glance at the person who had introduced himself into her room in this extraordinary manner.

He was a young man, some twenty-five or twenty-six years of age, and appeared to belong to the ranks of the people; he wore a Calabrian hat, round which a piece of velvet was tied, the ends of which fell loosely on his shoulders, a velvet vest with silver buttons, breeches of the same material, and ornamented in a similar manner; round his waist he wore a red silk belt with green fringe; shoes and leather gaiters completed his costume, which appeared to have been selected to set off his fine figure to advantage. His features possessed a kind of savage beauty, his look was bold and proud, his beard black, his teeth sharp and white, and his nose aquiline.

For a certainty, Gemma was not a whit the more easy by her examination, for the stranger, when he saw her stretch out her hand towards the table, as if to take hold of the silver bell, said—

"Did you not hear me, madame?" giving his voice that gentle expression so peculiar to the Sicilian dialect. "I wish you no harm—far from it. If you will grant me the request I am about to make, I will adore you as if you were a Madonna. You are already as beautiful; be as good as one."

"But what is it you require?" said Gemma, her voice still trembling; "and why did you come here in this manner, and at such an hour?"

"Had I requested the favour of au interview with one so noble, so rich, and so much loved by a man who is almost a king, is it probable that you would have granted it to me, so poor and unknown? Tell me, madame. But even if you had been so condescending, you might have delayed your answer, and I have no time to wait."

"What, then, can I do for you?" said Gemma, recovering herself by degrees.

"Everything, madame; for you hold in your hands my despair or my happiness—my death or my life."

"I do not understand you; explain yourself," faltered out the countess.

"You have," said the stranger, "a young woman from Bauso in your service."

"Teresa?" asked the countess.

"Yes, Teresa," replied the young man in trembling accents. "Now, this young woman is to be married to a valet de chambre of the Prince de Carini, and she is betrothed to me."

"Ah! it is you, then?" said the countess.

"Yes, it was I she was about to marry when she received your letter desiring her to come to you. She promised to

16

remain faithful to me—to mention me to you, and if you refused her request, she pledged her word to return to me. I continued to expect her; but three years passed by, and yet I saw her not; and as she has not returned to me, I have come to seek her. On my arrival I learnt all, and then I thought I would throw myself on my knees before you, and ask Teresa of you."

"Teresa is a girl I am partial to," said the countess, "and I do not wish her to leave me. Gaetano is the prince's valet de chambre, and by marrying him she will still remain near me."

"If that is one of the conditions, I will enter the prince's service," said the young man, evidently suppressing his feelings.

"But Teresa told me you would not enter into service."

"That is true," replied the stranger; "but if it is necessary, I will make any sacrifice for her; only, if it were possible, I would be one of the huntsmen rather than a domestic servant."

"Well," said the countess, "I will speak of it to the prince, and if he consents—"

"The prince will do all that you wish, madame," interrupted the young man. "You do not ask, you order; I know that well."

"But what guarantee have I for your good conduct?" asked the countess.

"My eternal gratitude, madame," said the young man.

"Still I must know who you are," said the countess.

"I am a man," said the stranger, "whom you can make miserable or happy; that is the sum of all."

"The prince will ask me your name," said the countess.

"What is my name to him?" asked the stranger. "Is he acquainted with it? Has the name of a poor peasant of Bauso ever reached the prince's ears?"

"But I belong to the same country as yourself," said the countess; "my father was Count of Castel Nuovo, and lived in a little fortress a quarter of a league from the village."

"I know it, madame," said the young man, in a low hoarse voice.

"Well, I ought to know your name," said the countess. "Tell me, then, and I will see what I can do for you."

"Believe me, madame la comtesse," said the stranger, "it would be better for you to remain ignorant of it. What does my name signify? I am an honest man. I would make Teresa happy; and if it were necessary, I would sacrifice my life for you or the prince."

"Your obstinacy is very strange," said the countess, "and I have a greater desire to know your name than ever, for when I asked Teresa what it was, she, like you, refused to tell me. In the meantime, I warn you that I will not consent to your wishes except on that condition."

"You wish to know it then, madame?"

"I insist upon it!" said the countess.

"For the last time," said the stranger, "I beg, I implore you, not to insist upon it."

"Either name it," said the countess, in an imperative tone, "or leave me."

"I am called Pascal Bruno," said the young man, in so calm a voice that you might have imagined every emotion had passed away if the paleness of his features had not been evidence of the internal struggle.

"Pascal Bruno!" cried the countess, drawing baek in her chair in terror. "Pascal Bruno! You, the son of Antonio Bruno, whose head is placed in an iron cage at the Château de Bauso?"

"I am his son," coolly replied the young man.

"And do you not know," asked the countess, "why your father's head is placed there? Speak!" Pascal remained silent. "Well," continued the countess, "it was because your father attempted to assassinate mine."

"I know all that, madame," replied Pascal, calmly; "and I know, besides, that when you, then a child, was taken into the village, your attendants showed you that head, and told you it was my father's head; but they did not tell you, madame, that your father dishonoured mine."

"Thou liest!" passionately exclaimed the countess.

"May God punish me if I tell not the truth. Madame, my mother was beautiful and virtuous; your father, the count, became enamoured of her: but she resisted all his importunities, all his promises, and all his threats; but one day, when my father had gone to Taormina, the count caused her to be carried off by four men, taken to a small house that belonged to him between Limero and Furnari (it is now a tavern), and there—madame—he violated her!"

"The count was lord and master of the village of Bauso," said Gemma, proudly. "Both the property and the persons of its inhabitants belonged to him, and he did your mother much honour by admiring her."

"My father did not think so it appears," said Pascal, knitting his brow. "That, perhaps, was because he was born at Stilla, on the lands of the Prince de Moncada Paterno; and on that account he struck the count. The wound was not mortal; so much the better. For a long time I deeply regretted it; but now, to my shame, I congratulate myself on it."

"If my memory be correct," said the countess, "not only was your father put to death as murderer, but your uncles are still at the galleys."

"Your memory is good," said Pascal. "My uncles gave an asylum to the assassin, and defended him when the officers came to arrest him: they were, therefore, looked upon as accomplices, and sent, my uncle Placido, to Favignana; my uncle Pietro, to Lipari; and my uncle Pépe, to Vulcano. As for myself, I was too young; and, although I was arrested, they gave me up again to my mother."

"And what became of your mother?" asked Gemma.

"She died," said Pascal, mournfully.

"Where?" asked Gemma.

"In the mountains between Pizzo di Goto and Nisi," replied Pascal.

"Why did she leave Bauso?" inquired the countess.

"That every time we passed the castle," said Pascal, "she might not see the head of her husband, nor I that of my father! Yes, she died without a physician, without a priest—she was buried in unholy ground, and I dug her grave. There, madame—you will pardon me, I trust—over the newly-turned earth I swore to avenge the wrongs of my family—of whom I, alone, remain—upon you, the only survivor of the family of the count. But I became enamoured of Teresa, and I left the mountains that I might not see my mother's grave, towards which I felt myself perjured. I came down to the plain, and went to Bauso. I did more than that, for when I knew that Teresa had left the village to enter your service, I thought of entering that of the count. For a long time I felt repugnant at the idea; by my love for Teresa overcame every other feeling. I made up my mind to see you—I have seen you; here am I, without arms, and a suppliant before you, madame—before whom I ought only to appear as an enemy."

"You must perceive," said Gemma, "the prince cannot take into his service the son of a man who was hanged, and whose uncles are at the galleys."

"Why not, madame?" asked Bruno, "if that man consents to forget that those punishments were unjustly inflicted?"

"Are you mad?" said the countess.

"Madame la comtesse," said Pascal, "you know what an oath is to a mountaineer. Well, I have broken my oath. You also know the vengeance of a Sicilian. Well, I will renounce my vengeance and forget my oath. I ask only that all may be forgotten, and that you will not force me to remember it?"

"But if you should," said the countess, "how would you act?"

"I do not wish to think upon the subject."

"Then we must take our measures accordingly," said the countess.

"I beg of you, madame la comtesse," said Pascal, "to have pity on me; you see that I am doing all that I can to remain an honest man. Once engaged by the prince—once Teresa's husband, I can answer for myself: otherwise I shall never return to Bauso."

"It is impossible to do as you desire," said the countess, decidedly.

"Countess," said Pascal, earnestly, "you have loved?" Gemma smiled disdainfully. "You must know what jealousy is—you must know its sufferings, its maddening tortures. Well, I love Teresa—I am jealous of her; and I feel I should lose my senses if this marriage take place; and then—"

"Well, then—" said Gemma, in an agitated tone.

"Then, take heed' I do not remember the galleys where my uncles are, the cage in which my father's head is placed, and the grave where my mother sleeps!" At this instant a strange cry, which seemed to be a signal, was heard outside the window, and almost at the same instant a bell was rung.

"There is the prince," said Gemma, regaining her confidence.

"Yes, yes—I know it," mattered Pascal; "but before he passes through yonder door, you have time to say 'yes.' I implore you, madame, to grant me what I ask. Give me Teresa—place me in the prince's service!"

"Let me pass," said Gemma, imperiously, and advanced towards the door; but instead of obeying this order, Brufio sprang to the door and bolted it. "Would you dare to stop me?" cried Gemma, taking hold of the bell. "Help! help!"

"Do not call out, madame," said Bruno, still mastering his feelings, "for I have told you I will do you no harm."

A second cry, resembling the first, was heard outside the window.

"It is well—well, Ali; you watch faithfully, my boy," said Bruno. "Yes, I know the count has arrived; I hear him in the corridor. Madame, madame! an instant longer remains for you; one second, and all the misfortunes I foresee may be avoided."

"Help, Rodolpho! Help!" screamed Gemma.

"You have, then neither heart, nor soul, nor pity, either for yourself or others," cried Bruno plunging his hands in his hair and looking at the door, which was being violently shaken.

"I am fastened in!" cired the countess, who felt fresh courage from the assistance which had arrived; "fastened in with a man who is threatening my life. Help! help! Rodolpho, help!"

"I do not threaten you," said Pascal, "I am entreating you—I entreat you still; but since you will—" Bruno, uttering a yell like that of a tiger, sprang upon Gemma, no doubt with the intention of strangling her, for (as we have said) he had no arms. At the same instant a small door, concealed at the extremity of the alcove, opened, the report of a pistol was heard, the room was filled with smoke, and Gemma fainted: when she recovered her senses she was in the prince's arms.

"Where is he? where is he?" she cried, in a terrified accent, and looking around her.

"I cannot tell; I suppose I must have missed him," answered the prince; "for, while I was stepping over the bed, he leaped out of the window; and, as I saw you insensible, I did not trouble myself about him—I thought only of you; I must have missed him, and yet it is strange I do not see the mark of the ball in the hangings."

"Let them run after him," said Gemma: "show no mercy, no pity, to that man, my lord, for he was a robber, who would have assassinated me."

They searched the villa during the whole night, the gardens, and the shore, but without avail—Pascal Bruno had disappeared.

The next day a track of blood was discovered, which began at the foot of the window from which he had leaped and was lost on the sea-shore.

CHAPTER II.—BRUNO AND ALI.

At daybreak the following morning, the fishermen's boats left the port as usual and dispersed themselves over the sea. In the meantime, one of their little fleet, having on board a man, and a boy of twelve or fourteen years of age, stopped when it came within sight of Palermo, and lowering its sail, brought to; but as this motionless state, at a spot little favourable for fishing, might have attracted suspicion, the boy occupied himself in mending his nets. As to the man, he was lying at the bottom of the boat, his head resting on the side, and he appeared to be plunged in a deep reverie, still, as if mechanically, he took up the sea-water with his right hand, and poured it over his left shoulder, which was bound up with a bandage stained with blood.

The man was Pascal Bruno, and the boy the same who, placed beneath the countess's window, had twice given him the signal for flight: at first sight, you could see that he was a native of a more ardent clime than that in which the events we record took place. He was born on the coast of Africa, and it was in the following manner that Pascal Bruno became acquainted with him:—

About a year before the occurrence of the events we have just narrated, a party of Algerine pirates, having learned that the Prince of Moncana Paterno, one of the richest noblemen in Sicily, was returning in a small vessel from Pantelleria to Catana with an escort of a dozen men only, lay in ambush behind the island of Porri, distant about two miles from the coast. The prince's vessel, as the pirates had foreseen, passed between the island and the shore, but the instant it entered the narrow strait, the pirates left the creek in which they had been concealed with three vessels and rowed forward to attack their expected prize, the prince. The latter, however, immediately perceiving the imminence of his danger, ordered his crew to turn the boat's head towards the shore, and run her aground on the beach at Furella. They did not succeed in reaching the point desired, but the place where the boat grounded had only about three feet of water, and the pirates were close upon them. The prince and his followers leaped into the sea, holding their arms above their heads, trusting to be able to reach a village they saw at some half a league distance without being obliged to employ them. But they had scarcely disembarked, when another party of the pirates who, having foreseen this manouvre, had rowed one of the boats as high as Bufaidone, issued from the reeds through which the river flowed, and cut off the retreat of the prince.

The attack immediately began, but while the followers of the prince were engaged with the first party, the second came up, and all resistance becoming evidently useless, the prince surrendered, asking for his life, and promising to ransom himself and all his followers. Immediately after the prisoners had laid down their arms, a party of countrymen were seen approaching, armed with muskets and pitchforks, and the pirates, having made themselves masters of the prince's person, the only object they had in view, did not think it worth while waiting for the arrival of the countrymen, but took to their boats in such haste as to leave behind them three of their men, whom they believed were either dead or mortally wounded.

Among those who had hastened to the scene of conflict, was Pascal Bruno, whose wandering life led him sometimes to one place and sometimes to another, his disturbed mind leading him into every kind of adventurous enterprise. When the countrymen reached the beach where the struggle had taken place, they found one of the Prince of Paterno's domestics dead, another slightly wounded in the thigh, and three of the pirates bathed in their blood, but still breathing. Two blows from the butt-end of a musket soon made an end of two of the number, and a pistol-ball was about to send the third to join his comrades, when Bruno perceiving it was a boy, turned the arm that held the pistol on one side, and declared that he would take the wounded lad under his own protection.

There were a few remonstrances against this ill-timed pity as it was called, but when Bruno had said a thing, he maintained what he had said; accordingly, he cocked his carbine, and declared that he would blow out the brains of the first man who should approach his protégé, and as they knew him to be a man who would not hesitate an instant in putting his threat into execution, they allowed him to take the boy in his arms and go off with him. Bruno proceeded to the shore, and entered the boat in which he performed his adventurous excursions, whose qualities he knew so well that it seemed to obey him like a well-tutored horse, and spreading his sail, he steered towards Cape Aliga Grande.

As soon as he saw that the boat was in the right course, and that it no longer needed a steersman, he attended to the wounded boy, who was still insensible: he took off the white bournouse in which he was dressed, loosened the belt to which his yataghan was still attached, and perceived by the rays of the setting sun the situation of the wound. Upon examination, he discovered that a musket-ball had entered between the right hip and the false ribs, and gone out near the spine: the wound was dangerous, but it was not mortal.

The evening breeze, and the cool sensation produced by the sea-water with which Bruno washed the wound, recalled the boy to his senses, and he uttered a few words in a foreign language, but without opening his eyes. Bruno, however, knowing that a wound caused by fire-arms produced a burning thirst, guessed that he was asking for drink, and he placed a bottle of water to his lips. The boy drank greedily, uttered a few inarticulate sounds, and fell back in a fainting fit.

Pascal laid him down as gently as he could at the bottom of the boat, and, uncovering the wound, he continued, unceasingly, to apply to it his handkerchief dipped in the sea—a remedy considered infallible in the case of wounds by every seafaring man in the Mediterranean.

At length our navigators found themselves at the mouth of the Ragusa, and the wind setting in from the African coast. Pascal with little difficulty directed his bark into the stream; and leaving Modica to the right, he passed the bridge that is thrown across the high-road from Noto to Chiaramonti.

He went about half a league further, but there the river became no longer navigable; he drew his boat up among the shrubs that grew by the side of the stream, and taking the boy in his arms, he carried him inland. He soon reached the entrance to a valley, into which he descended, and presently came to a spot where the mountain was perpendicular, the smoother side of which was pierced in various places; for in this valley were to be seen the remains of the habitations of the dwellers in caves, the first occupants of the country, and who were afterwards civilised by the Greeks.

Bruno entered one of these caverns, which communicated by means of a few steps with an upper story, to which the air was admitted through a small, square hole that answered the purpose of a window. A bed of rushes was heaped up in the corner, and on this he spread out the boy's bournouse; and then having lighted a branch of fir, he fixed it in the wall, and seating himself on a stone near the bed, he waited until his protégé recovered his senses.

This was not the first visit Bruno had paid to this retreat, for often during his travels across the island without any object in view, but merely for the sake of passing away his solitary time, he had entered that valley, and rested in that chamber which had been excavated in the rock three thousand years before. Here it was that he gave himself up to vague and incoherent reveries, so habitual to imaginative but uninstructed minds.

He knew that a race of men had disappeared from the earth

which in former times excavated these retreats; and, deeply tinged with the popular superstition, he believed, like all the inhabitants of the locality, that these men were enchanters and dealers in witchcraft; but this belief, far from driving him from these wild and terror-inspiring places, irresistibly attracted him to them; for in his youth he had heard numbers of tales related of enchanted guns, invulnerable men, and invisible travellers; and his fearless mind, delighting in the marvellous and the terrible, had but one engrossing desire, that of meeting with some mysterious being, some sorcerer, enchanter, or demon who, by means of an infernal compact, would endow him with some supernatural power, and make him superior to the rest of mankind. But he had vainly invoked the shades of the ancient inhabitants of the valley of Modica; no supernatural appearances had visited him, and Pascal Bruno remained, to his great regret, a man like other men, with the exception of a degree of strength and skill for which no other mountaineer could be compared with him.

Bruno had been wholly absorbed in one of these visionary reveries for nearly an hour beside the bed of the wounded lad, when the latter awoke from a species of lethargy into which he had been plunged, opened his eyes, looked round him with a wandering gaze, and at last fixed his eyes upon the man who had saved him, but unconscious whether he saw in him a friend or an enemy. During this examination, and by an indefinite instinct of self-defence, he put his hand to his waist In search of his faithful yataghan; but not finding it there, he heaved a deep sigh, and again closed his eyes.

"Are you in pain?" said Bruno to him, making use of the Lingua Franca, a language so well understood on the coast of the Mediterranean, from Marseilles to Alexandria, from Constantinople to Algiers, and by means of which you may travel over the whole of the old world.

"Who are you?" asked the boy.

"A friend," replied Pascal.

"I am not a prisoner then?" said the boy.

"No," answered Pascal.

"Then how came I here?" asked the boy.

Pascal told him all that had happened; to which the boy listened attentively, and when he had finished his tale, he fixed his eyes gratefully upon Pascal, and said, "Then, since you have saved my life, you will be a father to me?"

"Yes," said Bruno, "I will."

"Father," said the wounded boy, "thy son's name is Ali; what is yours?"

"Pascal Bruno."

"May Allah protect thee," said the lad.

"Are you in want of anything?" asked Bruno.

"Yes, water," said the boy; "I am thirsty."

Pascal took up an earthen vessel concealed in a hole in the rock, and went to a spring that flowed near the cave; on going up again he cast his eyes on the boy's yataghan, which he had made no attempt to draw nearer to him. Ali greedily seized the cup, and drank off the water at a draught.

"May Allah grant you as many happy years as there were drops of water in this cup," said the boy, as he gave it back to

31

Pascal.

"You are a good creature," murmured Bruno; "make haste and get well, and you shall, if you wish go back to Africa."

The boy recovered from his wound, but continued to remain in Sicily, for he became so much attached to Bruno that he would not leave him. Since that time, he had always remained with him, accompanying him in his hunting excursions over the mountains; assisting him in the management of his boat, and ready to sacrifice his life at a sign from the man he called his father.

On the previous evening, he had accompanied Pascal to the villa of the Prince de Carini, and waited for him beneath the windows during the interview with Gemma; and he it was who had twice given the signal of alarm; the first time, when the prince rang the bell at the gate, and again, when he entered the château. He was just about to climb into the window to render Bruno assistance when the latter sprang out; he followed him in his flight, and when they reached the shore, they both of them got into their boat which was awaiting them, and as they could not have put to sea in the evening without creating suspicion, they were content to remain among the fishing-boats that waited for the break of day, in order that they might put to sea.

During the night Ali, in his turn, returned to Pascal the attentions he had received under similar circumstances, for the Prince of Carini had taken a good aim, and the ball he had vainly searched for in the hangings had almost passed through Bruno's shoulder, so that Ali had but to make a slight incision with his yataghan to extract it from the side opposite to that at which it entered. All this took place without the interference of Bruno who appeared scarcely to pay any attention to the circumstance, and the only care he bestowed on his wound was, as we have already said, to moisten it, from time to time, with sea-water, while the boy appeared to be busy mending his nets.

"Father," said Ali, suddenly interrupting himself in his pretended occupation, "look towards the shore."

"Well, what is it?" said Pascal.

"A number of people?". replied Ali.

"Where?" asked Pascal.

"Yonder, on the road leading to the church," replied Ali.

In fact, a considerable crowd of people were passing along the winding road that led to the church. Bruno saw that it was a marriage procession on its way to the chapel of St. Rosalie.

"Direct the boat's head to the shore, and row quickly," he cried, starting up and standing in the boat.

The boy obeyed, seized the oars, and the little vessel seemed to fly over the surface of the sea; the nearer they approached the shore the more terrible the features of Bruno became: at length, when they were within half a mile of the land, he cried out, in an accent of deep despair—

"It is Teresa! They have hurried on the ceremony; they would not wait until Sunday for fear I should have carried her off. God knows, I have done all in my power to bring this affair to a happy conclusion—but they would not have it, so woe betide them!"

At these words, Bruno, assisted by Ali, hoisted the sail of his little bark, which, doubling Mount Pellegrino, disappeared at the end of two hours behind Cape Gollo.

CHAPTER III.—THE FATAL BRIDAL.

Pascal was not deceived in his conjectures: the countess, afraid of some attempt on the part of Bruno, had hurried on the marriage three days before the appointed time without informing Teresa of her interview with her old lover; and the young people had selected the chapel of St. Rosalie, the patroness of Palermo, for the celebration of the ceremony.

This was another of the characteristics of Palermo, that city of love; it had placed itself under the protection of a young and pretty saint! Thus, St. Rosalie was at Palermo what St. Januarius is at Naples, the omnipotent distributor of the blessings of heaven; but superior to St. Januarius, as she was of a royal French race, being descended from Charlemagne; this was proved by her genealogical tree, painted above the door on the exterior of the chapel; a tree whose trunk issues from the breast of the conqueror of Vitikind, and after dividing into many branches, it reunites at the summit to give birth to the Prince of Sinebaldo, the father of St. Rosalie; but her noble birth, the riches of her house and her own beauty had no effect on the young princess; at the age of eighteen she quitted the court, and, bent upon living a life of contemplation, she suddenly disappeared, and no one knew what had become of her; it was only after her death that she was found, as beautiful and perfect as if she still lived, in the grotto in which she had taken up her abode, and in the attitude in which she had fallen asleep. In after times, a chapel was erected over this grotto, and in this chapel Teresa and Gaetano were married.

The ceremony having concluded, the marriage procession returned to Palermo, where vehicles were in readiness to take the guests to the village of Carini, the princely fief from which Rodolpho took his title; there, by the care of the countess, a magnificent repast was prepared. The country people in the neighbourhood had been invited, and they had flocked to the feast from four or five leagues round. The tables were arranged on an esplanade, shaded by the foliage of green oaks and parasol-like firs, perfumed by orange and lemon trees, and surrounded by hedges of pomegranate and Indian fig-trees—a double blessing bestowed by Providence, who, providing for the hunger and thirst of the poor, has planted these fruitful trees like so much manna over the whole surface of Sicily.

This esplanade was reached by a road, the sides of which were planted with aloes, whose giant blossoms, seen from a distance, resembled the lances of Arab horsemen; while to the south, the view was bounded by the palace. Above the terrace, from which the chain of mountains rises that separate the island into three part—the eastern, northern, and western—at the extremity of these three valleys, the magnificent Sicilian sea was seen in three places; and, by its varying tints, it might have been taken for three distinct oceans; for, on account of the varied light produced by the sun just beginning to disappear in the horizon, on the side of Palermo it was an azure blue, round the Isoladette Donne it rolled its silvery waves, while it fell in golden streams against the rocks of St. Vito.

When the dessert was served, and while the guests were at the height of their joy, the gates of the château opened, and Gemma, leaning on the prince's arm, preceded by two servants carrying torches, and followed by a host of attendants, came down the marble staircase of the villa and went up to the esplanade. The peasants were about to rise, but the prince made a sign they should not disturb themselves; while Gemma and himself, having made the tour of the tables, stopped before the newly-married couple.

Then a domestic held out a golden cup, which Gaetano filled with Syracuse wine. The domestic then offered the cup to Gemma, and she uttered a prayer for the happiness of the bride and bridegroom, touched the wine with her beauteous lips, and offered it to the prince, who emptied it at a draught, and pouring into it a purseful of golden ducats, desired it to be given to Teresa, for whom it was a wedding gift. At the same instant, loud cries of "Long live the Prince of Carini! Long live the Countess of Castel Nuovo!" were heard; and at this moment the esplanade became illuminated as if by magic, and the noble visitors retired, leaving behind them, like a celestial vision, happiness and light.

They had scarcely re-entered the castle along with their suite before the music struck up, and the younger guests, leaving the table, proceeded to the place prepared for the dance. According to custom, Gaetano was about to open the ball with his bride, and for that purpose was advancing towards her, when a stranger, who had entered by the aloe walk, appeared on the esplanade—it was Pascal Bruno, in the Calabrian costume we have already described, excepting that he had a pair of pistols and a dagger at his girdle, and that his jacket, which was thrown over his right shoulder like that of a Hussar, exposed his shirt, stained with blood.

Teresa was the first who noticed him; she screamed, and fixing her terrified eyes upon him, remained pale and erect, as if she had seen a spectre; every one turned towards the new comer, and all were silent, anticipating some dreadful event.

Pascal Bruno went straight up to Teresa, and stopping before her, he folded his arms, and looked fixedly at her.

"Is it you, Pascal?" stammered Teresa.

"Yes, it is I," said Bruno, in a hoarse voice; "I heard at Bauso, where I was waiting for you, that you were about to be married at Carini, and I have come in time, I hope, to dance the first tarantella with you."

"It is the right of the bridegroom," observed Gaetano, going up to him and interfering.

"It is the right of the lover," replied Bruno. "Come, Teresa, I think it is the least you can do for me."

"Teresa is my wife," exclaimed Gaetano, extending his arm towards her.

"She is my betrothed," cried Pascal, taking her by the hand.

"Help! help!" exclaimed Teresa.

Gaetano seized Pascal by the collar, but at the same instant he uttered a loud cry and fell. Pascal's dagger was buried in his chest up to the hilt. The men appeared by their actions to be about to seize upon the murderer, who quietly drew a pistol from his waist and cocked it, then with the hand that held it, he made a sign to the musicians to play the tarantella; they obeyed mechanically, while all the guests remained motionless.

"Come, Teresa," said Bruno.

Teresa was no longer an accountable or conscious creature, but an automaton, whose actions were guided by fear—she mechanically obeyed, and the horrible dance, in the presence of the corpse of the murdered man, was danced to the last step.

At length the musicians stopped, and Teresa, as if the music alone had supported her, fell senseless on the body of Gaetano.

"Thanks, Teresa," said her partner, coldly, "that is all I wanted of thee," and then turning to the spectators, "and now, if any one desires to know my name, that he may find me elsewhere, I am called Pascal Bruno."

"Son of Antonio Bruno, whose head is placed in an iron cage at the château of Bauso?" asked one of the guests.

"Exactly so," answered Pascal; "but if you wish to see it, you must make haste, for I swear to you it shall not remain there much longer?"

At these words Pascal left, and no one felt inclined to follow him; besides, whether it arose from fear or interest, every one was engaged about Gaetano and Teresa; one was dead—the other mad!

The prince was not made acquainted with this terrible tragedy till the following morning, when every effort was made to capture the murderer, but in vain; he had escaped, no one knew how or whither.

The countess, in consequence of this dreadful event, became more alarmed than ever for her personal safety, particularly when she reflected that by her duplicity, in concealing from Teresa her extraordinary interview with Pascal, she herself had been the chief cause of the catastrophe.

The Sunday after this occurrence there was a fête at Bauso, and the whole village was full of life; there was drinking in every cabaret, and broaching of barrels at every corner; the streets were noisy and decorated with flags, and the chateau was thronged with people who had gathered together to see the young men fire at the target, an amusement much encouraged by King Ferdinand the Fourth during his forced sojourn in Sicily; and many of those who were, at the time we are speaking of, about to devote themselves to this exercise, had very recently, as followers of Cardinal Ruffo, had occasion to exhibit their skill against the patriots of Naples and the French republicans; but on this occasion it was merely a trial of skill, the prize being a silver cup.

The target was fixed immediately below the iron cage in which the head of Antonio Bruno was placed. The latter could only be reached by a flight of steps in the interior of the fortress, which led to a window, on the outside of which the cage was fixed.

The conditions of the shooting-match were simple

enough: to become one of the candidates it was only necessary to subscribe to the common purse, for the purpose of defraying the expense of the cup—the charge was two carlins for each shot, for which the party received in exchange a number, drawn by chance, which fixed the order in which each man was to fire. The least skilful took as many as ten, twelve, or even fourteen numbers; and those who reckoned on their superior skill not more than five or six.

In the midst of the confusion of drawing the numbers, a hand was stretched out among the rest which threw down two carlins, and a voice was heard asking for a single number. Every one turned round, astonished at this evidence either of poverty or confidence. The man who asked for a single number was Pascal Bruno.

Although he had not been seen in the village for four years, every one knew him, but still no one addressed him; but as he was known to be the best hunter in the country, they were not astonished at his asking for one number only—his number was eleven.

At length the firing commenced. Every shot was greeted by shouts of laughter or applause; but after the first few shots the laughter was less violent. As to Pascal, he was leaning sad and pensively on his English rifle, and seemed to take no part in the enthusiasm and merriment of his countrymen. At length it was his turn; they called his name, he started and raised his head as if the call was unexpected; but recovering himself at once, he took up his position behind a cord that was stretched across as a kind of barrier. Every one anxiously followed the direction of his eyes, for none of the marksmen had excited so much interest or had been watched so silently.

Pascal himself seemed to feel the importance of the shot he was about to take, for he fixed himself firmly, his left leg in advance, and resting his body on his right. He placed his gun carefully to his shoulder, and, beginning from below, he slowly raised the barrel; every one watched him with anxiety, and they saw, with astonishment, that his aim was above the target; but he still continued to raise his rifle, until it was in the direction of the iron cage. Then the rifle and the marksman remained for an instant motionless, as if they had been formed of stone; at length he fired, and the head rolled out of the cage to the bottom of the target. Every one shuddered, but no sound was heard at this proof of address.

In the midst of this silence, Pascal Bruno walked coolly up to the target, picked up his father's head, and without uttering a word or looking once behind him, he took the cross road that led to the mountains.

The spectators saw Bruno depart without attempting to stop or follow him; in fact, they commiserated the fate of Antonio Bruno, who was much respected by his fellow-villagers, and appreciated this act of filial affection in the son.

CHAPTER IV.—THE PRINCE AND THE BANDIT.

Scarcely a year had passed after the events we have just related before all Sicily—from Messina to Palermo—from Cephalu to Cape Passaro—was filled with reports of the exploits of the bandit Pascal Bruno. Considering the previous history of his family, his adventurous character, and the badly-organised state of society in his native country, it is not astonishing that Pascal Bruno should so rapidly have become the extraordinary character he desired to be. He had, as it were, established himself as a judge over justice itself; so that throughout all Sicily, and particularly at Bauso and its environs, no arbitrary act could be performed without escaping the notice of his tribunal; and as most of his judgments affected the powerful only, the weak were almost always on his side.

In this manner, when some rich lord imposed a heavy rent on a poor farmer—when a marriage was about to be broken off though the cupidity of a family—when an iniquitous sentence was passed on an innocent man—Bruno, after receiving notice, would shoulder his carbine, let loose his four Corsican dogs (his only band), mount his Valda Noto horse—half Arabian and half mountaineer, like himself—leave the little fortress of Castel Nuovo, where he had taken up his abode, go to the lord, the father, or the judge, and the rent was reduced, the marriage took place, or the prisoner was set at liberty.

From this, it may be very well understood, that all those men to whom he had thus been a benefactor would pay for the benefits they had received by devotion to his interests, and that every attempt made to capture him would be sure to fail, through the grateful watchfulness of the peasants, who warned him by signals agreed on beforehand of the dangers that threatened him.

Then, again, the most strange tales were told of him by everybody; for the simpler men's minds are, the fonder they are of believing the marvellous. They said, that on a stormy night, when the whole island trembled, Pascal Bruno entered into a compact with a sorceress, by which he obtained from her, giving his soul in exchange, the gift of being invisible, and the faculty of transporting himself in an instant from one end of the island to the other; as well as being rendered invulnerable, either by lead, iron, or fire. The bargain, they said, was to stand good for three years, Bruno having only signed it for the purpose of accomplishing an act of vengeance, for which purpose this term, short as it was, would be sufficient.

As for Pascal, far from destroying this belief, he perceived it was beneficial to him, and he endeavoured, on the contrary, to give it the appearance of truth. These various tales had often afforded him the means of establishing his invincible nature, by attributing to it a knowledge of circumstances which it must be imagined would otherwise have been perfectly unknown to him. The speed of his horse, by whose aid he could find himself in the morning at incredible distances from the place where he had been seen at night, convinced them of his locomotive faculty. A circumstance, also, of which he had taken advantage, like a skilful man, had left no doubt of his invulnerable nature; it was as follows:—

The murder of Gaetano had produced a great sensation; the Prince of Carini had given orders to all the commanders of companies to endeavour to arrest the assassin, who, however, led those who followed him a long chase through his audacity and cunning; they had, therefore, transmitted these orders to their agents.

The chief justice of Spadafora was informed, one morning, that Pascal Bruno had passed through the village during the night on his way to Divieto; the two following nights, therefore, he placed men in ambuscade on the road-side, thinking he would return by the same road he had taken when going, and take advantage of the night to perform his journey.

Wearied out by their two nights' watching, the morning of the third day, which was Sunday, the soldiers had assembled at a drinking-shop about twenty steps from the road-side: they were about to begin their breakfast, when some one brought them word that Pascal Bruno was quietly coming along the road from the direction of Divieto: as they had no time to conceal themselves, they waited for him where they were, and when he was within fifty yards of the inn, they sallied out and drew up before the door, without, however, appearing to notice him. Bruno, on his side, saw these preparations for the attack without any apparent uneasiness, and, instead of retracing his steps, an easy task, he put his horse into a gallop and continued his journey. As soon as the soldiers perceived his intention, they got their muskets ready, and the moment he passed before them, the whole company saluted him with a general discharge; but neither horse nor rider was touched, and they emerged safe and sound from the cloud of smoke in which they had been for an instant enveloped. The soldiers looked at them and shook their heads, and proceeded to recount what had happened to the judge of Spadafora.

The report of this adventure reached Bauso the same evening; and several of the inhabitants, whose imagination was more lively than that of their neighbours, began to think Pascal Bruno was enchanted, and that lead and iron when they struck him became soft and flattened. The next day this assertion was proved by incontestable evidence; for they found his jacket at the justice's door, pierced in thirteen places by bullets, and the thirteen flattened balls were found in one of the pockets. Some unbelievers, however, and among them was Caesar Alletto, a notary of Calvaruso, from whose lips we had these particulars, maintained that the bandit himself, having miraculously escaped from the volley of musketry, and wishing to profit by the circumstance, had hung his jacket to a tree and pierced it with bullets in thirteen places. But, notwithstanding this opinion, the majority were convinced of his bearing a charmed life, and the terror Pascal already inspired was considerably increased.

This dread of Bruno was so great and so well established that, spreading from the lower orders, it had infected even the higher classes, and to such an extent that, a few months before the time at which we have arrived, being in want of two hundred ounces of gold for one of his philanthropic projects (it was to rebuild an inn which had been burnt down), he addressed himself to the Prince of Butera to obtain a loan of the money, describing to him a place in the mountains where he would go to receive it, and begging of him to bury it at the precise spot, so that on the night he mentioned he might go and seek it. In case this request, which, however, more resembled a command, was not attended to, Bruno warned the prince there would be open war between the king of the mountains and the king of the plains; but that if, on the contrary, the prince would be kind enough to lend it to him, the two hundred ounces of gold would be faithfully returned out of the first money he should be able to carry off from the royal treasure.

The prince of Butera was one of those characters which have become extremely rare in modern times: he was one of the ancient Sicilian nobility, as adventurous and chivalrous as the Normans, by whom their constitution and society were formed. His name was Hercules, and he seemed formed after the model of that ancient hero. He could knock down a restive horse with a blow of his fist; break a bar of iron, half an inch thick, on his knee; and bend a piastre with his finger. An occurrence, in which he had exhibited the greatest presence of mind, had made him the idol of the people of Palermo. In 1770, there was a scarcity of bread in the city; a riot was the consequence; the governor had appealed to the ultima ratio, and the cannon were drawn out in the Toledo street; the people were moving towards the guns; the gunner, with match in hand, was in the act of firing on the people, when the Prince of Butera seated himself over the mouth of a cannon, as coolly as if it had been a chair, and in that situation made so eloquent and rational a speech that the mob dispersed of its own accord, and the gunner threw away the match, and the gun returned into the arsenal innocent of human blood. But this was not the only cause of his popularity.

He was in the habit every morning of walking on his terrace, which overlooked the Place de la Marine, and as the gates of his palace were open to everybody, at daybreak he always found a number of poor people assembled; on that account he constantly wore a huge buckskin waistcoat, whose immense pockets were filled every morning by his servant with carlins and half-carlins, all of which, to the very last piece, disappeared during his walk, and that with words and actions that belonged to himself alone, so that he always seemed as if he was about to knock down those on whom he was bestowing charity.

"Your excellency," said a poor woman, surrounded by her family, "have pity on a poor mother with five children."

"An excellent reason," replied the prince, in an angry tone; "am i their father?" and shaking his fist in her face, he dropped a handful of money into her apron.

"My lord prince," said another, "I am without food."

"You fool," replied the prince, giving him a cuff, and at the same time enough to procure him food for a week; "do I make bread? Why do you not go to the baker's?"

On this account, whenever the prince passed along the street every head was uncovered, and if he had said the word, he might have been made King of Sicily; but that idea never entered his head, and so he remained Prince of Butera.

This liberality of his, however, met with a reprover, and that within the walls of the prince's palace, and this reprover was his major-domo. It is clear that a man with a character like that we have endeavoured to trace must necessarily keep a splendid table; in fact, he kept in every sense of the word open house, so that every day he had from five-and-twenty to thirty guests at the least to dine with him; among these, seven or eight were perfect strangers to him; while, on the other hand, there were others who seated themselves as regularly as boarders at a table d'hôte.

Among these last there was a certain Captain Altavilla, who had gained his epaulettes by following Cardinal Ruffo from Palermo to Naples; and who returned from Naples to Palermo with a pension of a thousand ducats. Unfortunately, the captain was somewhat of a gambler, and this would have caused his pension to be insufficient for his wants, if he had not discovered two plans by means of which his quarterly pay had become the least important part of his revenue; the first of these plans, and one, as I have already said, that was open to all the world, was to dine every day with the prince; and the second was, every day, with the most scrupulous regularity, to put the silver cover of the plate off which he had dined into his pocket.

The manouvre continued for some time before this daily abstraction was noticed; but, well furnished as the plate-chests of the prince might be, they began to exhibit certain vacant spaces. The suspicions of the major-domo immediately fell on the follower of Cardinal Ruffo; he, therefore, carefully watched him, and after two or three days his suspicions were changed into certainty.

He immediately informed the prince of the discovery he had made, who reflected for an instant, and then answered, that so long as the captain merely took his own cover he should take no notice; but that if he put his neighbour's into his pocket, why then he would consider how he would act. In consequence of this, Captain Altavilla continued to be one of the most regular guests of his excellency Prince Hercules de Butera.

The prince was at Castrogiovanni, where he had a villa, when Bruno's letter was brought to him. He read it, and asked if the messenger was waiting for an answer. He was told, "no" and immediately he put the letter into his pocket, with as much sang froid as if it had merely been on some trivial subject.

The night fixed upon by Bruno had arrived; the spot he had indicated in his letter was on the southern ridge of mount Etna, near one of the numerous extinct volcanoes that were indebted for their existence of a day to its eternal fires—an existence, nevertheless, sufficient for the destruction of cities. The volcano in question was called Montebaldo; for each of these terrible hills received a name at the time it was raised up from the earth. Ten minutes' walk from its base a colossal and isolated tree arose, called the chesnut of a hundred horses, because around its trunk, the circumference of which is equal to 178 feet, and beneath its foliage, which of itself forms a forest, a hundred horsemen and their steeds can take shelter.

It was at the root of this tree Bruno was to seek the money he wished to borrow of the prince; consequently, about eleven o'clock in the evening he left Centorbi, and towards midnight he began to discern by the light of the moon the gigantic tree, and the small house built between its stems, in which its immense produce is harvested. As he drew near, Pascal thought he could distinguish a shadow cast upon one of the five trunks which arose from the same root. Soon afterwards the shade appeared a reality; the bandit stopped, cocked his carbine, and cried, "Who goes there?"

"A man, to be sure!" exclaimed a powerful voice. "Why, zounds! you did net expect the money could come alone?"

"No, certainly not," said Bruno; "but I did not think the man who brought it would have been bold enough to wait for my coming."

"Then you are not acquainted with Prince Heretics de Butera? that is all."

"How! yourself my lord?" said Bruno, throwing his carbine over his shoulder and advancing hat in hand to the prince.

"Yes, it is I, you rogue," replied the prince; "I, who thought a bandit might be in want of money the same as any other man; and I did not wish to refuse my purse even to a bandit,

51

only I took the fancy of bringing it myself for fear he should imagine I was afraid of him."

"Your excellency is worthy of your high reputation," said Bruno.

"And you, are you deserving of yours?" asked the prince.

"It depends upon how I have been spoken of to your excellency," said Bruno, "for I have more than one reputation."

"Good," continued the prince; "I see you are not deficient in ability or resolution; I admire brave men, let me meet with them where I will. Listen to me; will you change your Calabrian dress for the uniform of a captain and fight against the French? I will raise a company for you on my own estates, and purchase your epaulettes."

"Thank you, my lord, thank you," said Bruno, "your offer is like that of a magnificent prince; but I have a certain act of vengeance to accomplish that will keep me for some time longer in Sicily; after that we shall see."

"Well," said the prince, "you are free; but, believe me, you had better accept my offer."

"I cannot, your excellency," said Bruno.

"Well then," said the prince, "here is the money you asked for; go to the devil with it, and take care you don't get yourself hanged on the gibbet opposite my door on the Place de la Marine."

Bruno balanced the purse in his hand.

"It seems to me that the purse is very heavy, my lord," said he.

"That is because I did not wish a fellow like you should

be able to brag that he had fixed a limit to the liberality of the Prince of Butera; so, instead of the two hundred ounces of gold you asked for, I have put three hundred in the purse."

"Whatever sum you have been pleased to bring, my lord, it shall be faithfully returned to you," said Bruno.

"I give; I never lend," said the prince.

"And I borrow or I steal—I never beg," replied Bruno; "take back your purse, my lord, I shall address myself to Prince Ventimille, or to Prince de la Cattolica."

"Well, let it be so," said the prince; "I never met with a more capricious bandit: four rascals like you would drive me mad; so I shall leave. Farewell!"

"Adieu, my lord!" said Bruno, "and may St Rosalie protect you."

The prince departed, with his hands in the pockets of his buckskin waistcoat, and whistling a favourite air; Bruno remained motionless watching his departure, and it was not until he had lost sight of him that he, on his side, retired, heaving a deep sigh.

The next day, the innkeeper whose house had been burned down received, by the hands of Ali, the Prince of Butera's three hundred ounces of gold.

CHAPTER IV.—THE ROBBER'S CASTLE.

Some time after the event we have just related, Bruno learnt that a convoy of money, escorted by four gens-d'armes and a brigadier was about to leave Messina for Palermo; it was the ransom of the Prince Moncada Paterno; which, in consequence of a financial operation, which did great honour to the imagination of Ferdinand the Fourth, had just helped to swell the Neapolitan budget instead of increasing the treasure of Casuba, according to its first destination.

The following is the history of the transaction, as it was told me in Sicily, and, as it is as curious as it is authentic, we think it deserves the trouble of being told; besides, it will give some idea of the simple manner in which taxes are imposed in Sicily.

We have already related the manner in which the Prince de Moncada Paterno was made prisoner by the Barbary Corsairs near the little village of Tugello, on his return from the island of Pantalleria. He was carried, along with all his followers, to Algiers, and there the price of his ransom and that of his attendants was modestly fixed at the sum of five hundred thousand piastres (about one hundred thousand pounds sterling), half to be paid before his departure, and the other half after his return to Sicily.

The prince wrote to his steward to inform him of the situation in which he found himself placed, and desired him to send, as quickly as possible, the two hundred and fifty thousand piastres in exchange for which he was to be liberated. As the Prince of Moncada Paterno was one of the richest noblemen in Sicily, the sum was easily made up and sent to Africa; and faithful to his promise, like a true follower of the prophet, the Dey released the Prince of Paterno, taking his word of honour that before a year had passed by he would remit the remaining two hundred and fifty thousand piastres.

The prince returned to Sicily and endeavoured to collect the sum necessary for the second instalment of his ransom in his own principality, when an order came from Ferdinand IV., who, seeing that he was at war with the regency, had no wish that his subjects should enrich his enemies; he therefore opposed the proceedings of the prince, and ordered the two hundred and fifty thousand piastres in question to be paid into the treasury at Messina.

The Prince of Paterno, who was a man of honour a well as a faithful subject, obeyed the order of his sovereign and the voice of his conscience at the same time, so that his ransom cost him seven hundred and fifty thousand piastres, two-thirds of which were sent to the infidel Corsair, and the other third placed at Messina in the hands of the Prince de Carini, the agent of the Christian pirate. This was the sum the viceroy was sending to Palermo, the seat of government, under the escort of four gens-d'armes and a brigadier; the last being likewise charged with the duty of delivering a letter from the prince to his dear Gemma, whom he requested to join him at Messina, where the business of government would still detain him for several months.

On the evening when the convoy would have to pass near

Bauso, Bruno unfastened his four Corsican dogs, crossed the village, of which he had become the lord, in their company, and placed himself in ambuscade on the road between Divieto and Spadafora. He had remained there about an hour, when he heard the wheels of a waggon and the tramp of horsemen. He looked to the priming of his carbine, satisfied himself that his dagger was not fixed in its sheath, whistled to his dogs, who laid themselves down at his feet, and remained standing upright in the middle of the road.

A few minutes afterwards, the convoy appeared at a turning in the road, and advanced to within fifty paces of the man who was waiting for its coming up. When the gens-d'armes perceived him, they hailed him with, "Who goes there?"

"Pascal Bruno," replied the bandit; and, at the sound of a peculiar whistle, his powerful dogs, trained for the purpose, fiercely attacked the little troop.

At the name of Pascal Bruno, the four gens-d'armes had taken to their heels, and the dogs by natural instinct pursued the runaways. The brigadier, who remained alone by the waggon, drew his sabre and rushed at the bandit. Pascal raised his carbine to his shoulder as coolly and slowly as if he were about to shoot at a mark, determining not to fire until the horseman was within ten paces of him; but the instant he placed his finger on the trigger, and before he had time to fire, both horse and man rolled in the dust. Ali had stealthily followed without saying a word to Bruno, and seeing the brigadier about to charge him, he had crawled along the road like a serpent and cut the horse's hamstrings with his yataghan. As to the brigadier, his fall was so rapid and unexpected that his head struck against the stones, and he was rendered totally insensible.

Bruno went up to him, after satisfying himself that there was no feint attempted to be practised upon him, and with the assistance of Ali he placed him in the waggon he had so lately escorted; then placing the reins in the hands of the young Arab, he desired him to take the waggon and the brigadier to the fortress. Bruno himself then went up to the wounded horse, took the brigadier's carbine from the saddle, to which it was attached, and searched in the holsters and took out a roll of paper which he found there; he then whistled to his dogs, who returned with their mouths covered with blood, and followed the capture he had just made.

When he arrived in the court-yard of his little fortress, he closed the gate behind him, took the brigadier (who was still insensible) on his shoulder, carried him into a room, and placed him on a mattress on which he was in the habit of throwing himself with all his clothes on; then, whether through forgetfulness or imprudence, he placed the carbine he had taken from the saddle in a corner, and left the room.

Five minutes afterwards the brigadier opened his eyes, looked round, and found himself in a place that was completely unknown to him; and, believing he was under the influence of a dream, he felt round him to ascertain whether he was really awake. It was then that he felt a pain in his forehead, and placing his hand on it, he withdrew it covered with blood: he found that he was wounded. The wound brought back his recollection, and he remembered he had been stopped on the road by a single man, deserted in a most cowardly manner by the gens-d'armes who accompanied him, and that at the instant he was about to attack that man his horse suddenly fell; beyond that he could recall nothing to his mind.

The brigadier was a brave man, but he felt that the responsibility of this disastrous adventure rested on him, and his heart was filled with shame and rage at the disgraceful conduct of his men. He looked round the room to discover if possible where he was; but everything was strange to him. He rose, went to the window, and saw that it overlooked the country. It was then that a ray of hope entered his breast, for he could easily leap out of the window, go in search of assistance, and return and avenge himself upon his captor.

He had just opened the window for the purpose of executing his project when, casting a parting glance into the chamber, he perceived his carbine standing near the head of the bed; at this unexpected sight his heart beat violently, for other thoughts besides those of flight instantly took possession of his mind. He looked round to ascertain whether he was really alone, and when he was satisfied that no one had seen or could see him, he seized the weapon, in which he saw a more hazardous means of safety, but a speedier vengeance. After having ascertained that the priming was safe, and finding, by passing the ramrod down the barrel, that it was loaded, he replaced it where he had found it, and lay down as if he had not as yet recovered his senses; but he had scarcely stretched himself out on the mattress before Bruno entered the room.

He had a piece of lighted fir in his hand, which he threw into the fire-place, where he set fire to the wood already placed there for the purpose; then he went to a cupboard formed in the wall, and took out two plates, two glasses, two flasks of wine, and a roast shoulder of mutton, which he placed on the table, and appeared to be waiting until the brigadier recovered his consciousness that he might do the honours of the repast.

The room in which the scene we are narrating took place was longer than it was wide, having a single window at one end, a single door at the other, and the chimney between the two. The brigadier, now a captain of the gens-d'armes at Messina, who has given us all these particulars, was lying down, as we have said, parallel to the window; Bruno was standing before the fire-place, with his eyes vaguely fixed on the door, and he appeared to become every instant more and more thoughtful.

This was the moment for which the brigadier was waiting—the decisive moment when he must stake everything for one object—life against life, head against head. He rose, resting upon his left hand, and stretched out his other slowly towards his carbine, but without taking his eye off Bruno; he took hold of it between the lock and the butt-end, and then remained an instant in that position without daring to make another movement, alarmed even at the beating of his own heart, which was so violent that the bandit might almost have heard it had he not been so entirely lost in thought; then, seeing that he gave himself up to his fate as it were, he resumed his confidence, rose on one knee, looked once more at the window, his only means of retreat, placed the carbine to his shoulder, took aim at Bruno like a man who knew that his life depended on his self-possession, and fired.

Bruno quietly stooped down, picked up something that lay at his feet, held the object to the light, and, turning towards the brigadier, who remained mute with astonishment—

"Comrade," he said, "when next you attempt to shoot me let your balls be of silver, for unless they are they will be only flattened against me in this manner. However, I am happy you have so far recovered yourself, for I begin to feel hungry; we will, therefore, if it is agreeable, sit down to our supper."

The brigadier remained in the same attitude in which he had fired, his hair bristling on his head, and the perspiration standing in thick drops on his forehead. The next instant the door opened, and Ali, yataghan in hand, rushed into the room.

"It is nothing, my boy, nothing," said Bruno; "the brigadier discharged his carbine, that is all; make yourself easy, and go to rest; have no fear for me."

Ali left the room without answering, and went and laid himself down across the first door-way upon the panther's skin that served him for a bed.

"Well," continued Bruno, turning towards the brigadier and filling the two glasses with wine, "did you not hear me?"

"I did," replied the brigadier, rising, "and since I have not been able to kill you, were you the very devil himself, I would drink with you."

Uttering these words, he walked boldly up to the table, took up the glass, touched the brim of Bruno's, and drank off the wine at a draught.

"What is your name?" asked Bruno.

"Paolo Tommassi, brigadier of gens-d'armerie, at your service," was the reply.

"Well, Paolo Tommassi," continued Bruno, placing his hand on his shoulder, "you are a brave fellow, and I have a great inclination to make you a promise."

"What is it?" asked the brigadier.

"To let no one but you," said Bruno, "obtain the reward of three thousand ducats that is set upon my head."

"That is an excellent idea," observed the brigadier.

"Truly so; but it must first come to maturity," said Bruno; "in the meantime, as I am not yet tired of my life, take a seat, and let us sup; and we will talk the matter over by-and-by."

"May I cross myself before I eat?" said Tommassi. "Certainly," replied Bruno.

"I thought it might, perhaps, be unpleasant to you," said the brigadier; "we are not always sure."

"Anything you like," said Bruno.

The brigadier made the sign of the cross, seated himself at the table, and attacked the shoulder of mutton like a man whose conscience was perfectly at ease, and who knew that he had done, under very difficult and trying circumstances, all that a brave soldier could do. Bruno kept him nobly in countenance; and, certainly, to see these two men seated at the same table, drinking out of the same bottle, and helping themselves from the same dish, no one would have imagined that each in his turn had, within the last hour, done all he could to kill the other.

For an instant they were both silent, partly on account of the important business in which they were engaged, and partly from the preoccupation of their minds. Paolo Tommassi was the first to give utterance to the double idea on which his mind was engaged.

"Comrade," he said, "you live well here; it must be allowed you have excellent wine, certainly, and you do the honours of the table like a right-good fellow; but I acknowledge I should enjoy all this much better if I knew when I was to leave here."

"To-morrow morning, I presume," replied Bruno. "You will not keep me here as a prisoner, then?" asked the brigadier, eagerly.

"A prisoner! why what the devil should I do with you here?" asked Bruno.

"Hem!" said the brigadier, "so far it is not so bad; but—" he continued, evidently embarrassed, "that is not all."

"What else is there?" said Bruno, filling the brigadiers glass.

"Why—is—" said the brigadier, holding his glass up before the lamp; "it is rather a delicate question, you see."

"Go on," said Bruno; "I am listening."

"You will not be angry, I hope, at what I am about to say?"

"I think you ought to know my character better by this time," said Bruno.

"True, true, you are not irritable, I know that well," said the brigadier. "I am speaking about a certain waggon—there, now its out."

"That is down in the court-yard," observed Bruno, holding his glass up to the light in his turn.

"I am rather doubtful," replied the brigadier; "but you understand me, I cannot go without my waggon."

"Very well, then, you shall take it with you," said Bruno.

"Untouched?"

"Hum!" said Bruno; "it will not be much short, considering the sum it contains. I shall only take what I am absolutely in need of."

"Are you in want of much?" asked the brigadier, with anxiety.

"I want three thousand ounces," said Bruno.

"Well, that is reasonable enough," said the brigadier; "a good many people would not be so delicate as you are."

"You may make yourself quite easy in the matter, for I will give you a receipt for what I take," said Bruno.

"Talking of receipts," said the brigadier, rising, "that's well thought of, for it reminds me of some papers I had in my holsters."

"Don't make yourself uneasy about them," observed Bruno; "here they are."

"You will do me the greatest service by returning them to me," said the brigadier.

"I know that," said Bruno, "for I have satisfied myself of their importance; the first is your brigadier's commission; I have made a note at the foot of that, declaring that you have conducted yourself so well that you deserve to be made a quarter-master. The second is my description, and I have taken the liberty to make a few small corrections as to particular signs; for instance, I have added charmed: the third paper is a letter from his excellency the viceroy to the Countess Oemma, of Castel Nuovo; and I have too much gratitude for this lady, who has lent me this castle of hers, to place any restraint on her loving correspondence. Here are your papers, my brave fellow; one more glass to your health, and sleep tranquilly. To-morrow, at five o'clock, we will put you on your road; it is much more prudent, I can assure you, to travel by day than by night, for perhaps you may not always have the good fortune of falling into such good hands."

"I think you are right," said Tommassi, rolling up his papers, "and you appear to me to be an honester fellow than many more apparently honest folks of my acquaintance."

"I am happy to leave you with such favourable impressions on your mind," said Bruno, "you will sleep the more pleasantly; by-the-by, I must give you one caution, do not go down into the court-yard, or my dogs might by chance make a meal of you."

"Thank you for the caution," said the brigadier. "Good-night," exclaimed Bruno, and he went out of the room, leaving the brigadier to continue his supper, or go to sleep till the hour appointed for his departure.

Next morning at five o'clock, according to agreement, Bruno entered his guest's chamber, whom he found up and ready to start, he conducted him down stairs, and led him to the gate; there was the waggon, together with a magnificent horse, and all the harness that belonged to the animal Ali's yataghan had rendered unserviceable. Bruno begged of his friend, Tommassi, to accept of this present as a keepsake. The brigadier was too well pleased to allow the offer to be made twice; he therefore mounted his new steed, started the team in the waggon, and left quite delighted with his new acquaintance.

Bruno watched his departure, and when he was about twenty paces off, he cried out, "Above all, do not forget to give the beautiful Countess Gemma the Prince of Carini's letter."

Tommassi made a sign with his head and disappeared round the corner of the road.

And now, if our readers wish to know how Pascal Bruno was not killed by the discharge of Tommassi's carbine, we will give them the answer we received from Signor Caesar Aletto, the notary of Calvaruso: it is, that it is probable that on the road to the fortress, the bandit took the precaution of removing the bullet from the carbine. But Paolo Tommassi always considered that it was a much simpler explanation to attribute it to magic.

We give our readers both these opinions, and they are at perfect liberty to adopt that which suits them best.

CHAPTER VI.—A BANDIT'S GRATITUDE.

It may well be imagined that the report of exploits like these were not confined to the little village of Bauso: it was the general theme of conversation among all classes. Nothing was talked of in all Sicily but the brave brigand who had taken possession of the Castel Nuovo, and who, from thence, like an eagle from his eyry, swooped down upon the plain, sometimes to attack the great, and at others to assist the weak: thus he was always on the popular side. Our readers will, therefore, not be astonished that our hero's name was heard pronounced at the palace of Prince Butera, who had given a splendid entertainment at his mansion, the Place de la Marine.

Knowing the character of this prince, we can easily guess what a fête must be when given by him. The one in question, however, exceeded in splendour the ideas of the most fertile imagination. It was like an Arabian Nights' dream, and the remembrance of it is perpetuated in Palermo, although Palermo is a fairy city, and is still celebrated for its unsurpassed magnificence.

Imagine the most splendid saloons lined with mirrors from the ceiling to the floor, some leading to trellised walks, from the summit of which the richest grapes of Syracuse and Lipari were hanging; others to ample square spaces, surrounded by beautiful orange and pomegranate trees, covered with blossoms and fruit at the same time: these spaces were devoted to dancing English and French dances.

As to the waltzers, they wound their mazy career round two immense marble reservoirs, from each of which sprang up beautiful jets of water, which, from the reflection of many-coloured lamps, by which the whole was illuminated, fell like glittering showers of diamonds. From these delightful spots long alleys issued, sprinkled with golden-coloured sand, and leading to a little hill, surrounded with silver vessels, containing every refreshment that could be desired, and overhung by trees covered with crystal instead of natural fruits: finally, on the summit of this hill, and facing the paths that led to it, was a buffet in four divisions, constantly replenished by means of some internal mechanism. To render the whole more fairylike and enchanting, the musicians were invisible, and the sound alone of their instruments reached the ears of the guests. It might indeed have been supposed to be a fête given by the genii of the air.

At the same time, to animate these magical decorations, you must imagine the most beautiful women and the most elegant cavaliers of Palermo dressed in costumes each exceeding its neighbour in splendour and singularity—each with a mask on the face or in the hand, breathing the balmy air, intoxicated with the invisible harmony, and dreaming or talking of love; but even then, you would be far from drawing a picture of this night equal to that preserved in the memories of those that were present when I passed through Palermo thirty-two years after it took place.

Among the groups that wandered through the alleys and saloons, there was one beyond all others which attracted the attention of the crowds; it was that which followed in the train of the beautiful Countess Gemma, and which she drew after her as a planet does its satellites. She had but that instant entered, accompanied by five others, who, like herself, had assumed the costume of the thirteenth century—a dress so simple and elegant, and which, at the same time, appeared to be expressly chosen to set off the figure to advantage, and she advanced in the midst of a murmur of admiration, led by the Prince de Butera himself, who, disguised as a mandarin, received her at the entrance, and preceded her to present her, as he said, to the daughter of the Emperor of China.

As it was imagined that our Amphytrion intended some new surprise, they all followed the prince eagerly, and the cortège increased at every step it took.

He stopped at length at the entrance of a pagoda guarded by two Chinese soldiers, who, at a given signal, opened the door of an apartment entirely furnished with foreign objects, in the midst of which seated on a kind of chair, and dressed in a magnificent Chinese costume, which alone had cost thirty thousand francs, was the Princess de Butera, who rose as soon as she saw the countess approach, followed by a cloud of officers, mandarins, and attendants, each more dazzling, fierce-looking, or droll than his neighbour. This apparition had something so Eastern and fantastic in it, that the whole assemblage, accustomed as they were to luxury and magnificence, uttered an exclamation of astonishment. They surrounded the princess, touched her robe, embroidered with precious stones, shook the golden bells in her pointed hat, and for an instant the attention of the assembly was withdrawn from the beautiful Gemma and entirely centred in the lady of the house. Every one complimented and admired her, and among those who uttered the most exaggerated praise was Captain Altavilla, whom the prince had continued to receive at his dinner parties, to the great discomfiture of his major-domo, and who had dressed himself in full uniform for the purpose, it may be, of disguise.

"Well," said the Prince of Butera to the Countess of Castel Nuovo; "what do you think of the daughter of the Emperor of China?"

"I must say," replied Gemma, "that it is a happy thing for His Majesty, Ferdinand IV., that the Prince of Carini is at Messina at this moment, for he might be induced, with a heart like his, out of regard for the daughter, to give up Sicily to the father, and we should be obliged to have another Sicilian Vespers against the Chinese."

At this instant, the Duke of Moncada Paterno, in the dress of a Calabrian bandit, went up to the princess.

"Will her highness permit me," said the duke, "as a connoisseur, to examine her magnificent costume?"

"Sublime daughter of the sun," said Captain Alta-villa, pointing to the prince, "take care of your golden bells, for I warn you, that you have to do with Pascal Bruno."

"The princess," exclaimed a voice, "would be safer in the company of Pascal Bruno than in that of a certain follower of Cardinal Ruffo of my acquaintance; Pascal Bruno is a murderer, not a thief—a bandit, and not a cutpurse."

"Well answered," observed the Prince of Butera.

The captain bit his lips.

"By-the-by," said the Prince de la Cattolica, "have you heard of his last exploit?"

"Whose?" asked the Duke of Moncada.

"Pascal Bruno's," said the prince.

"No; what has he done?" asked the duke.

"He has stopped a convoy of money sent by the Prince of Carini to Palermo," replied the prince.

"My ransom!" exclaimed the duke.

"By heaven!" said the prince, "your excellency will, after all, be sacrificed to the infidels."

"Zounds! the king will surely not require me to have a second reckoning with him," replied Moncada.

"Let your excellency be reassured," said the voice which had just before addressed Altavilla; "Pascal Bruno only took three thousand ounces from the two hundred and fifty thousand piastres belonging to King Ferdinand IV."

"And how do you know that, my young Albanian?" said the Prince de la Cattolica, who was close by the speaker—a handsome young man, from twenty-six to twenty-eight years of age, and dressed in the costume of Vina.

"I have heard it reported," said the Greek, carelessly, and playing with his yataghan; "besides, if your excellency wishes for particulars, here is a person who can give them to you."

The party thus pointed out to public curiosity was no other than our old acquaintance, Paolo Tommassi, who, strict in the performance of his duty, had immediately on his arrival repaired to the Countess de Castel Nuovo's residence; but not finding her there, and hearing of the fete, he took advantage of his situation as envoy from the viceroy to enable him to gain admission to the gardens of the Duke de Butera.

In an instant he found himself in the centre of an immense circle and subjected to a thousand questions; but Paolo Tommassi was, as we have seen, a bold fellow, and was not easily put out of countenance: he, therefore, commenced by delivering the prince's letter to the countess.

"Prince," said Gemma, after having read the missive she had received, "you never suspected you were giving me a farewell fête; the viceroy orders me to proceed to Messina, and being a faithful subject, I shall begin my journey to-morrow. Thanks, my friend!" she continued, turning to Paolo Tommassi and handing him her purse; "you may now retire."

Tommassi endeavoured to take advantage of this permission of the countess, but he was too closely surrounded to make good his retreat easily; he was, consequently, obliged to surrender at discretion—the condition of his liberty being an exact account of his recent encounter with Pascal Bruno.

He related it, it must be acknowledged, with all the simplicity of real courage; he told his auditors, without any superfluous addition, how he had been made prisoner; how he was taken to the fortress of Castel Nuovo; how he fired at the bandit without the ball taking any effect; and how, finally, the latter sent him away, making him a present of a magnificent horse in exchange for that which he had lost.

Everybody listened to this tale, which bore the impress of

truth, with the silent attention of belief, with the exception of Captain Altavilla, who raised some doubts as to the veracity of the honest brigadier; but, luckily for Paolo Tommassi, the Prince de Butera himself came to his assistance.

"I will lay a wager," he said, "that nothing can be more true than what the brigadier has told us, for all the details appear to me to be perfectly in accordance with the character of Pascal Bruno."

"You know him, then?" said the Prince de Moncada Paterno.

"I do. I was in his company one night," replied the Prince de Butera.

"And where was that?"

"On your estates."

It was now the prince's turn; he related how Pascal and he had met at the chesnut of a hundred horses; how he, the Prince of Butera, had offered him a company, which he had refused; and, finally, how he had lent him three hundred ounces of gold.

At this last information, Altavilla could not restrain his mirth.

"And you think, my lord," said he, "that Bruno will bring them baek?"

"I am certain of it," replied the prince.

"Now we are on this subject," interrupted the Princess of Butera, "is there any one else in this company who has seen Pascal Bruno, and who has spoken to him? I doat upon tales of brigands, they make me ready to die with fright."

"There is the Countess of Castel Nuovo," observed the Albanian; "she has seen him."

Gemma started, and every one looked at her as if to interrogate her.

"Can it be true?" said the prince, turning towards her.

"Yes," said Gemma, trembling; "but I had forgotten it."

"He remembers it," muttered the young man.

All the company pressed round the princess, who in vain endeavoured to make excuses; she in her turn was obliged to relate the scene with which we opened this tale to tell how Bruno entered her chamber; how the prince fired at him; and how the bandit, to avenge himself, entered the villa on the nuptial day and killed Teresa's husband. This history was the most terrible of all, and it produced a deep sensation in the minds of the listeners; something like a shudder ran through the whole assembly, and had it hot been for the dresses of the guests, you would hardly have thought you were present at a fête.

"On my honour," said Captain Altavilla, who was the first to break silence, "the greatest crime the bandit has committed is in rendering this fête so melancholy; I could have pardoned him all his other misdeeds; but for this I swear, by my epaulettes, I will have vengeance; and from this moment I devote myself to his pursuit."

"Do you speak seriously, Captain Altavilla?" said the Albanian.

"Yes, on my honour!" replied the captain; "and I here declare there is nothing I so much wish for as to meet him face to face."

"That is not impossible," observed the Albanian, coolly.

"To the man who will render me that service," said the captain, "I will give—"

"It is useless to offer a reward, captain," interrupted the young man; "I know a man who will render you that service for nothing."

"And when can I meet with this man?" repeated Altavilla, affecting a smile of doubt.

"If you will follow me, I will tell you," replied the stoical Albanian.

With these words the Albanian withdrew, as if he were inviting the captain to follow him.

The captain hesitated for au instant, but he had said too much to draw back; all eyes were turned upon him, and he saw that the least show of timidity would ruin his reputation; and besides, he considered the proposal was a joke.

"Come on," he cried, "for the honour of the ladies and he followed the Albanian.

"Do you know who that young lord disguised as a Greek is?" said the countess, with a trembling voice, and addressing the Prince de Butera.

"No, on my soul, I do not," said he. "Does any one here know him?"

Everybody looked, but no one answered.

"With your permission," said Paolo Tommassi, carrying his hand to his hat; "I know him."

"And who is he, my brave brigadier?"

"Pascal Bruno, my lord," replied Tommassi.

The countess screamed and fainted away; and this incident put a sudden end to the fête.

An hour afterwards, the Prince de Butera had retired to his chamber, and, seated in front of his desk, was arranging some papers, when his major-domo entered.

"What's the matter, Jacomo?" asked the prince.

"I always told you so, my lord," said the major-domo.

"Well, what have you always told me?" asked the prince.

"That your goodness would only encourage him," replied Jacomo.

"Who do you mean?" asked the prince.

"Captain Altavilla," replied Jacomo.

"What has he done?" asked the prince.

"What has he done, my lord?" said Jacomo. "First, your excellency' will recollect I apprised you of his regularly putting his silver cover in his pocket."

"Well, go on," said the prince.

"I beg your pardon," said Jacomo; "but your excellency answered, that so long as he only pocketed his own, nothing was to be said."

"I recollect I said so perfectly well," said the prince.

"Well, my lord," said Jacomo, "to-day, it seems that he has not only taken his own, but his neighbours' also, for there are eight missing."

"Ha! that's quite another affair," said the prince; "I must communicate with him on the matter."

He took a sheet of paper, and wrote the following note:—

"Prince Hercules de Butera has the honour of informing Captain Altavilla, that as he no longer dines at home, and being by this fortuitous circumstance deprived of the pleasure of seeing him as previously, he begs he will accept the trifle he sends herewith as a small indemnity for the change this determination must make in his arrangements."

"Stay," continued the prince, giving the major-domo fifty ounces (twenty-six pounds sterling), "take this money, and deliver it and the letter to-morrow to Captain Altavilla."

Jacomo, who knew it was no use speaking after the prince had decided, bowed and left the room. The prince continued quietly arranging his papers when, at the end of about ten minutes, hearing a noise at the door of his room, he raised his head, and saw a man dressed as a Calabrian peasant standing on the threshold, with his hat in one hand and a bundle in the other.

"Who is there?" said the prince.

"I, my lord," replied the peasant.

"And who are you?" asked the prince.

"Pascal Bruno," replied the visitor.

"And what do you come for?" asked the prince.

"First, my lord," said Pascal Bruno, advancing and emptying his hat full of gold on the desk; "first, I have brought you the three hundred ounces you so kindly lent me: they were employed for the purpose I mentioned to you—the inn that was burnt down has been rebuilt."

"Ah, ah! you are a man of your word," said the prince; "well, I am glad of it."

Pascal inclined his head.

"Then," he added, after a short pause, "I have brought you back eight silver covers, with your arms and cypher on them, which I found in the pocket of a certain captain who, most likely, robbed you of them."

"Zounds," said the prince, "it's singular they should be brought back by you; and now, what have you in that bundle?"

"In this bundle," said Bruno, "is the head of a wretch who abused your hospitality, and which I have brought you as a proof of my sworn devotion to your service."

Saying this, Pascal Bruno untied the handkerchief, and taking the head of Captain Altavilla by the hair, he placed it, all bleeding as it was, on the duke's desk.

"What the devil am I to do with such a present as this?" said the prince.

"What you please, my lord," replied Pascal Bruno, who bowed and left the room.

The Prince of Butera remained alone for an instant with his eyes fixed on the head, balancing himself in his arm-chair, and whistling his favourite tune; he then, after an instant, rang the bell, and his major-domo made his appearance.

"Jacomo," said the prince, "it is of no use going to Captain Altavilla's to-morrow morning; tear up the letter; keep the fifty ounces, and throw this carrion on the dung-heap."

CHAPTER VII.—A BRIGAND'S VENGEANCE.

At the time of which we are speaking—that is, about the beginning of the year 1804, Sicily was almost in an uncivilised state, from which the return of King Ferdinand and its occupation by the English have partially emancipated it. At the present day, the road which now leads from Palermo to Messina, passing through Taormina and Catana, was not formed, and the only one that existed, we do not say good, but practicable to go from one capital to the other, was that which, passing along the sea-coast, went through Termini and Cephalu; abandoned for its new rival, it is at present scarcely frequented, except by artists in search of the magnificent prospects it discloses at every turn. The only mode of travelling on this road, on which no post was established, was formerly, as at present, on the back of a mule, in a litter carried by two horses, or in your own carriage, relays of horses being sent on before, and placed at every fifteen leagues.

So that the Countess Gemma de Castel Nuovo, when about to leave for Messina, at which place the Prince of Carini had written to her to join him, was obliged to choose one of these three modes. Travelling on a mule was too fatiguing for her, and a journey in a litter, besides the inconveniences of this mode of transport, the principal of which was its slow progress, was apt to produce a feeling like sea-sickness. The countess therefore decided, without any hesitation, in favour of the carriage, and sent forward relays of horses to four stations on the road, that is, to Termini, Cephalu, Saint Agatha, and Melazzo.

Besides these precautions, the courier was ordered to lay in a store of provisions at each of these spots, for the inns are so notoriously deficient in the necessaries of life, that every traveller is advised when he leaves Messina to provide himself for the journey—to purchase cooking utensils, and to hire a cook; to these preparations an experienced Englishman on one occasion added a tent, on account of the deplorable state of the houses of entertainment.

I know not whether it was a learned man, acquainted with ancient Sicily, or a shrewd observer who thoroughly understood modern Sicily, for whom they were at this instant preparing supper at the sign of the Cross, the inn which had been rebuilt with the Prince of Butera's three hundred ounces, and situated on the road from Palermo to Messina, between Ficara and Patti.

The activity of the innkeeper and his wife, who, under the directions of a foreign cook, were at the same time engaged upon fish, flesh, and fowl, proved that the man for whom the culinary apparatus was in requisition was determined not only to have enough, but had no objection to a superfluity.

He came from Messina, travelling in a carriage, and with his own horses. He had stopped because the situation of the inn pleased him, and having extracted from his trunk everything the most experienced traveller could require—linen, plate, even bread and wine—he was led into the best room, where he lighted some perfumed pastilles in a silver vase, and waited till his dinner was ready, seated on a rich Turkey carpet, and smoking the finest Mount Sinai tobacco in his amber chibouk, carelessly caressing at the same time a magnificent Corsican dog of the largest size that was lying at his feet.

He was attentively observing the wreaths of sweet-scented smoke as they escaped from his lips and condensed themselves on the ceiling, when the door of the apartment opened, and the host, followed by a domestic in the countess's livery, appeared on the threshold.

"Your excellency," said the worthy man, bowing to the ground.

"What's the matter?" asked the traveller, but without turning his head, and in a decided Maltese accent.

"Your excellency," said the host, "it is the Countess Gemma, of Castel Nuovo."

"Well!" replied the traveller.

"Her carriage has been obliged to stop at my poor inn," said the host, "because one of her horses became so lame that she is unable to proceed."

"Well, go on," said the traveller.

"She had calculated," said the host, "having no expectation of this accident when she left St. Agatha this morning, on sleeping at Melazzo this evening, where she has relays, so that she is entirely unprovided with everything."

"Tell the countess that my cook and larder are at her service," said the traveller.

"A thousand thanks in my mistress's name," said the

servant; "but as the countess will, no doubt, be obliged to pass the night in this inn, while a relay of horses is brought hither from Melazzo, and as she is equally unprovided for night as for day, she would be glad to know if your excellency would have the gallantry to—"

"More than that," said the traveller; "let the countess occupy my apartment—this room will do for her lady's-maid, whom she will not be sorry to have near her. As for myself, I am a man accustomed to fatigue and privations; I will content myself with the first room that is disengaged; go, therefore, and tell the countess she can step up at once—the room is at liberty, and our worthy host will do the best he can for me."

Speaking thus, the traveller rose, whistled to his dog, and followed the host; and the servant at once descended to accomplish his mission.

Gemma accepted the traveller's offer as a queen would the homage of a subject, and not as a woman who accepts a service from a stranger; she was so accustomed to see everything submit to her will, and everybody obey her voice, and even her look, that she saw nothing striking in the extreme gallantry of the traveller.

It is true she looked so beautiful as she moved towards the apartment, resting on the arm of her attendant, that every one bent before her. She was dressed in a most elegant riding-habit, fitting tightly over the arms and bust, and ornamented with silk braiding. For fear of the cold air of the mountains, she wore round her neck a beautiful sable boa, purchased by the Prince Carini of a Maltese merchant who had brought it from Constantinople. On her head she wore a little black velvet hat, of a fanciful shape, like the head-dresses worn in the middle ages; and her long and magnificent tresses hung down in ringlets after the English fashion. But, prepared as she was to find a room ready to receive her, she could not avoid being astonished when she entered at the elegant manner in which the traveller had concealed the poor appearance of the apartment.

All the utensils of the toilet were of silver, the cloth that covered the table was of the finest texture, and the oriental perfumes burning on the mantelpiece seemed fit for a harem.

"See, Gidsa, am I not predestined?" said the countess; "an awkward servant shoes my horses badly, I am obliged to stop, and my good genius, who finds me in this state of embarrassment, builds a fairy palace for me on the road."

"Has madame la comtesse," said Gidsa, "no suspicion who this good genius may be?"

"Really none," said the countess.

"It seems to me," said the waiting-maid, significantly, "that madame la comtesse ought to be able to guess!"

"I swear to you, Gidsa," said the countess, falling into a chair, "that I am in a state of perfect ignorance. Come, what are your ideas on the subject?"

"My ideas?" said the girl. "Madame, I trust you will pardon me, although my ideas are very natural."

"Oh! certainly," replied the countess; "speak as you think."

"I think," said the girl, "that perhaps his highness the

viceroy, knowing that your ladyship was on the read, had not patience to wait for your arrival, and"—

"Your idea," said the countess, "is amazingly good; indeed, it is more than probable. Besides, who, if it were not he, would have arranged a room like this for the purpose of giving it up to me? Now listen, you must say nothing if Rodolpho is preparing a surprise for me. I would give myself up entirely to it; I would not lose one of the emotions his unexpected presence would occasion me. It is agreed, therefore, that it is not the viceroy, but that the stranger is an unknown traveller; so keep your probabilities to yourself, and leave me in my state of doubt; besides, if it should be him, I shall have divined his presence, not you. How kind my dear Rodolpho is to me! how he foresees everything! Oh! how much he loves me!"

"And the dinner," said Gidsa, "that has been prepared with so much care; do you believe that the result of mere accident?"

"Chut! I believe nothing; I profit by the good things heaven has sent me, and I thank God for them. See what a lucky thing it is that this plate is here! if I had not met with this noble traveller, how should I have been able to eat off anything else? Look at this silver goblet, you might say it was engraved by Benvenuto. Give me some drink, Gidsa."

The attendant filled the goblet with water, and then added a few drops of Lipari malvoisie, and the countess sipped it, apparently more for the purpose of carrying the cup to her lips than because she was thirsty; it seemed as though, by the sympathetic touch of her lips, she endeavoured to discover whether it really was the man who loved her who had thus provided for the wants of a woman accustomed to all that luxury and magnificence which becomes almost an essential necessary to those who have been used to it from infancy.

Supper was served, and the countess ate like a fine lady, that is, tasting of all, like the humming-bird, the bee, or the butterfly; but, full of thought and anxiety, while she was eating, she kept her eyes constantly fixed on the door, and started every time it opened—her bosom was oppressed and her eyes moist; at length, she fell by degrees into a delicious state of languor for which she herself could not account. Gidsa perceived it and became uneasy.

"Is your ladyship unwell?" asked the anxious attendant.

"No," replied Gemma, in a feeble voice; "but do you not find these perfumes extremely oppressive?"

"Does your ladyship wish me to open the window?" asked Gidsa.

"No, no," replied the countess, "pray do not; I seem as if I should die, but death appears to be so sweet. Take off my hat, it feels so heavy, I cannot bear it."

Gidsa obeyed, and Gemma's long hair hung down in ringlets nearly to the ground.

"Do you feel like me, Gidsa," asked the countess, "an incomprehensible feeling of pleasure? A kind of heavenly sensation flows through my veins: I must have drank a charmed philter; help me to rise, and lead me to the mirror."

Gidsa supported the countess and led her towards the

mantelpiece; when she reached it, she rested both elbows upon it, placed her head in her hands, and looked at her beautiful face in the glass.

"Now, let everything be taken away, then undress me, and leave me alone."

The attendant obeyed her mistress; the servants of the countess cleared the table, and when they had left, Gidsa performed the second part of her mistress's orders, who still remained before the glass, merely raising her arms languidly one after the other, to make it just possible for her maid to perform the necessary duties, which were in a short time accomplished—the countess still remaining in the species of ecstacy into which she was plunged; then, as her mistress had directed her, she went out and left her alone.

The countess completed the remainder of her toilet in a state resembling somnambulism; she retired to rest, and remained for an instant leaning on her elbow, with her eyes fixed on the door; then by degrees, and notwithstanding all her efforts to keep awake, her eyelids became heavy, her eyes closed, and she sank upon her pillow, heaving a long deep sigh, and murmuring Rodolpho's name.

The next morning, when she awoke, Gemma stretched out her hand as if she expected to find some one by her side; but she was alone, and for a few minutes her eyes wandered round the chamber, and then turned and fixed themselves on the table by the bedside. An open letter lay upon it, she took it up and read:—

"Madame la Comtesse,—I could have taken the

vengeance of a brigand upon you; I preferred to indulge myself in the pleasure of a prince! but that, when you awake, you may not imagine you have been in a dream, I have left you a proof of the reality; look in your mirror.

"Pascal Bruno."

Gemma's whole frame shuddered, and a cold perspiration covered her forehead; she stretched out her arm towards the bell-rope that she might call for assistance, but womanly instinct arrested her arm, and collecting all her strength, she sprang out of bed, ran to the glass, and uttered a cry of horror. Her hair and eyebrows were completely shorn!

She hastily dressed herself, and enveloping her head in her veil, threw herself into her carriage, and ordered it to be driven back to Palermo.

The instant she arrived there, she wrote to Prince Carini, telling him that her confessor, as an expiation for her sins, had ordered her to shave off her eyebrows and hair, and retire for twelve months to a convent.

CHAPTER VIII.—-TREACHERY.

On the 1st of May, 1805, there was a high festival at Castel Nuovo: Pascal Bruno was in excellent humour, and gave a supper to one of his best friends, Placido Tomaselli, an honest dealer in contraband, belonging to the village of Gesso, and to two females the latter had brought with him from Messina. This delicate attention sensibly effected Bruno, and that he might not be behindhand in politeness with so provident a comrade, he determined to perform the honours of his domicile after the fashion of the best society. Accordingly, the finest wines of Sicily and Calabria were selected from the cellars of the fortress, the most noted cooks of Bauso were placed in requisition, and all that singular luxury was displayed to which at times it pleased the hero of our history to resort.

The guests had only just begun dinner when Ali brought Placido Tomaselli a letter, which a countryman from Gesso had placed in his hands. Placido read it, and crumbling it up in a violent passion, exclaimed—

"Upon my word he has chosen his time very nicely."

"What is it, comrade?" said Bruno.

"Perdition! why, a summons from Captain Luigi Cama, of Villa San Giovanni."

"What, our purveyor of rum?" asked Bruno.

"Yes," replied Placido; "he informs me he is off the shore, and has a full cargo which he wishes to dispose of before the custom-house officers hear of his arrival."

"Business before all things," replied Bruno. "I'll wait for you. I am in very good company, so make yourself easy; if you are not too long gone, you will find everything you leave, and more than you can take away."

"It is only an hour's work," replied Placido, appearing to yield to the reasoning of his host; "the beach is only about five hundred yards from this spot."

"And there is the whole night before us," observed Pascal.

"A good appetite, comrade," said Placido. "A successful expedition, master," said Bruno. Placido left the castle, and Bruno remained with the two women, and, as he had promised his guest, proceedings did not suffer by his absence. Bruno was amiable enough for any two, and the conversation began to assume the most animated character, when the door opened, and a new actor appeared on the scene. Pascal turned round and recognised the Maltese merchant we have already spoken of several times, of whom he was one of the best customers.

"By St. Gregory!" he exclaimed, "you are welcome; and the more so, if you haye brought any of those Turkish pastilles, a packet of Latakia tobacco, and a few Tunisian shawls; by-the-by, your opium acted admirably."

"I am glad of it," replied the Maltese; "but on this occasion, I have come on quite another business."

"Ah! you have come to sup with me, is that it?" asked Bruno. "Pray sit down, sit down, and once again you are welcome; there, that is a seat fit for a king."

"Your wine is excellent, I know, and these ladies are

charming," replied the Maltese; "but I have something very important to speak to you about."

"To me?" asked Bruno.

"Yes, to you," replied the Maltese.

"Well go on," said Bruno.

"I must speak to you alone," said the Maltese.

"Well, then," said Bruno, "I'll hear you tomorrow, my worthy captain."

"But I must inform you immediately," said the Maltese.

"Well, then, speak before the company," said Bruno; "we have not too many here, and I make it a rule when I feel comfortable never to disturb myself, even if my life were at stake."

"That is the very subject I wish to allude to," said the Maltese.

"Bah!" replied Bruno; "heaven looks after honest men; here's to your health, captain."

The Maltese emptied his glass.

"That's right; now sit down and let me hear your sermon, we'll listen to you with proper attention."

The merchant perceived he must give in to the whim of his host, and he consequently obeyed him.

"Well, now then, what is it?" said Bruno.

"First, then," continued the Maltese, "you know that the justices of Calvaruso, Spadafora, Bauso, Saponara, Divito, and Domita have been arrested."

"I have heard something about it," said Pascal Bruno, carelessly, at the same time emptying his glass of Marsala, the best wine in Sicily.

"But do you know the cause of their arrest?" inquired the merchant.

"I guess at it," said Bruno; "is it not because the Prince of Carini, being in an extremely ill-humour on account of his mistress having retired to a convent, has taken it into his head that they have been too slow, and have shown too little skill in their attempts to arrest a certain Pascal Bruno, whose head is worth two thousand ducats?"

"Exactly so," said the merchant.

"You see," said Bruno, "I am quite aware of what is going on."

"Yet, for all that," said the Maltese, "there may be some circumstances of which you are still ignorant."

"God is great! as Ali says," replied Bruno; "but go on, and I will acknowledge my ignorance; I wish for nothing so much as instruction."

"Well," said the Maltese, "the six judges have met together, and each has put down twenty-five ounces—that makes one hundred and fifty ounces."

"Or, in other words," replied Bruno, in the same careless tone, "eighteen hundred and ninety livres. You see, if my books are not well regulated, it is not for want of arithmetic. Well, what next?"

"After that," continued the merchant, "they offered this sum to two or three men, known as your common associates, if they would assist them in capturing you."

"Let them offer it," said Bruno; "I am quite certain they

will not meet with a traitor within ten leagues."

"You deceive yourself," answered the Maltese; "the traitor is found."

"Ha!" exclaimed Bruno, knitting his brow and grasping his dagger; "and how do you know that?"

"Why, my good fellow," said the merchant, "in the simplest way in the world; yesterday I was at the house of the Prince de Goto, governor of Messina, who sent for me for the purpose of purchasing some Turkish goods, when a servant entered the room and whispered a few words in his ear. 'Very well,' said the prince, 'let him come in.' He then made a sign to me to go into an adjoining room for a short time; I obeyed, and as he never suspected that I was acquainted with you, I overheard a conversation that concerned you."

"Well," said Bruno.

"It was the traitor," said the Maltese; "he undertook to open the doors of your fortress, and to place you in their hands unarmed while you were at sapper; and he himself engaged to conduct the gens-d'armes to your dining-room."

"And do you know who this man is?" demanded Bruno.

"Yes," said the merchant.

"His name?" said Bruno.

"Placido Tomaselli."

"Confusion!" exclaimed the bandit; "he was here but an instant ago."

"And has he left the castle?" inquired the merchant.

"Just before you came in," replied Bruno.

"Then," said the merchant, "he has gone after the police

and the soldiers; for, as far as I can see, you were about to sit down to supper."

"You see I was," said Bruno.

"Then I am right; and if you wish to escape, you have not a minute to lose."

"I fly!" cried Bruno, laughing. "Ali! Ali!" and Ali entered the room.

"Close the gates of the castle, my lad, and turn three of my dogs loose in the court-yard, and send the fourth, Lionna, upstairs, and get the ammunition ready."

The women began to scream.

"My goddesses, you must be quiet," observed Bruno, with an imperative look; "we must have no singing here; silence, and instantly, if you please."

And the women were silent.

"Captain, you must keep these ladies company; for my part, I must go my rounds."

Bruno seized his carbine, buckled on his cartouche-box, and went towards the door; but as he was about to leave the room he stood still and listened.

"What is the matter?" said the Maltese.

"Do you not hear my dogs bark? The enemy is close at hand; they were not long behind you;—are they not fine beasts? Silence, my tigers!" continued Bruno, opening one of the windows and giving a peculiar whistle; "all right, all right, I am on my guard."

The dogs gave a low growl and were then silent.

The women and the Maltese trembled with terror,

expecting something dreadful was about to happen, and at the same moment Ali entered the room with Pascal's favourite bitch, Lionna: the noble creature went straight up to her master, reared up on her hind legs, and placing her paws on his shoulders, she looked intelligently at him and gave a short bark.

"Yes, yes, Lionna, you are a fine beast," said Bruno, patting the dog fondly on the head; "come on, my beauty, come along."

And he went out, leaving the Maltese and the two women in the supper apartment.

Pascal went down into the court-yard, where he found the three dogs evincing great uneasiness, but without giving any indication that the danger was very pressing; he then opened the garden door and began to walk round its bounds. Suddenly Lionna stopped,' snuffed the air, and walked straight up to one part of the enclosure: as soon as she reached the wall, she reared up on her hind legs, as if she intended to scale it, grinding her teeth, and uttering a low growl, at the same time looking back at her master: Pascal Bruno was close behind her.

He was at once aware that an enemy was concealed, and that at no great distance, and recollecting that the window of the room in which Paoli Tomassi had been confined directly overlooked this spot, he ran quickly up stairs, followed by Lionna, who with open throat and fiery eyes seemed to guess her master's intention; and crossing the room in which the two women and the Maltese were anxiously awaiting the end of the adventure, she went into an adjoining chamber, in which there was no light and the window was open. She had scarcely entered when, crouching quietly on the ground, she crawled like a serpent towards the window, and when within a few feet of the casement, before Bruno could prevent her, she sprang through the opening like a panther, and alighted on the ground without injury, although the height was at least twenty feet.

Pascal was at the window nearly as soon as the dog; he saw her make three bounds towards an olive-tree, and then heard a cry of agony: Lionna had seized a man by the throat, who was concealed behind the tree.

"Help! help!" exclaimed a voice, which Pascal recognised as that of Placido. "Help, it is I! Call off your dog, or she will tear me to pieces."

"Hold him, Lionna!" exclaimed Bruno, "kill him, my good dog! Death to the traitor!"

Placido at once saw that Bruno had discovered all, and uttering a cry of pain and rage, a mortal combat ensued between the dog and the man. Bruno, resting on his carbine, calmly contemplated this singular duel by the uncertain light of the moon. He could perceive two bodies, whose forms were indistinct, struggling, rolling on the ground, and rising again, and seeming as if they were but one: for the space of ten minutes he heard their confused cries, but could not distinguish those of the dog from the man. At the end of that time a dreadful cry was heard, and one of them fell to rise no more—it was the man.

Bruno whistled to Lionna, again crossed the supper-room, without uttering a word, and went rapidly down stairs to open the door to his favourite bitch; but at the very instant she entered, bleeding from wounds inflicted with a knife, and even from the bites of her antagonist, he saw the musket-barrels of soldiers glittering in the rays of the moon, and advancing up the road that led from the village to the fortress. He at once barricaded the door, and again entered the room in which he had left his trembling guests. The Maltese was drinking, and the women saying their prayers.

"Well!" said the Maltese.

"Well, captain?" answered Bruno.

"What has become of Placido Tomaselli?" asked the merchant.

"His business is settled," replied Bruno; "but there is another legion of devils coming upon us."

"And what do you mean next to do?" asked the merchant.

"Kill as many as I can in the first instance," said Bruno.

"And then?" inquired the merchant.

"Fire the fortress," said Bruno, coolly, "and then—blow myself up along with the rest."

The women hearing this began to scream most lustily.

"Ali," said Pascal, "take these ladies into the vaults, and give them all they ask for except a candle, for fear they should set fire to the powder before the proper time."

The poor terrified creatures fell on their knees.

"Come, make haste!" cried Bruno, stamping his feet; "do as I order you."

And he uttered these words with such a look and accent, that the two girls rose and followed Ali without daring to utter another word of complaint.

"And now, captain," said Bruno, as soon as they were gone, "put out the lights, and get into some corner where the bullets cannot reach you; for the musicians have arrived and the ball is about to begin."

CHAPTER IX.—THE SIEGE.

A few moments after, Ali again entered the room, carrying on ids shoulders two or three muskets of the same calibre, and a basket full of cartridges. Pascal Bruno opened all the windows, that he might be able to face in any direction, and Ali, taking a musket in his hand, was about to place himself at one of them.

"No, my boy," said Pascal, in an affectionate and parental tone of voice, "that is no one's duty but mine; I have no wish to attach your fate to mine; I do not wish to drag you into the surf along with me; you are young; nothing, as yet, has removed your life out of the beaten track; take my advice, continue to live like the rest of the world."

"Father," replied the youth, with his gentle voice, "why do you not wish me to defend you as Lionna did? You know I have none to look to but you in the world, and that, if you die, I must die with you!"

"No, Ali," said Bruno, "if I die, I shall perhaps leave behind me some mysterious and terrible mission to be accomplished, which I can trust to no one but my child; my boy, therefore, must live to do what his father commands him."

"It is right," said Ali; "the father is the master, and the child must obey."

Ali seized Pascal's hand, and kissed it.

"Can I be of no service to you, father?" observed the lad.

"Yes; load the guns," said Bruno, and Ali addressed himself to the task,

"And what can I do?" said the Maltese, from the corner in which he had ensconced himself.

"You, captain? you shall have the task of carrying the flag of truce if it be needful."

At this instant Pascal Bruno saw the muskets of a second troop descending the mountain: they advanced in so direct a line towards the isolated olive-tree, at the foot of which lay the body of Placido, that it was evident it was the appointed place of rendezvous.

Those who marched first stumbled over the corpse. Upon this they formed a circle round it; but no one could recognise it, the teeth of Lionna had so much disfigured it; however, as it was at this olive-tree Placido had appointed a meeting, and as the body was at its foot, and no other living being in the neighbourhood, it was evident that the dead man was Placido himself.

The soldiers accordingly guessed that their plot had been discovered, and, consequently, that Bruno was on his guard; they, therefore, began to consider how they should act.

Pascal, standing at the window, watched all their movements; but the moon issuing suddenly from behind a cloud, a ray of light fell upon his figure, and one of the soldiers seeing him, pointed him out to his comrades.

"The bandit! the bandit!" was heard from all the troops, and a volley of shot was instantly poured in at the window.

A few of the balls flattened themselves against the wall, others whistled past the ears and over the head of the party at whom they were directed, and lodged in the mouldings of the ceiling.

Pascal replied by discharging four muskets in succession as they were handed to him by Ali: four men fell.

The soldiers, who were not troops of the line, but a kind of national guard organised for the protection of the high road, hesitated a little when they saw death pay them so sudden a visit; for all the men, reckoning on Placido's treason, had entertained the hope of making an easy capture: instead of which, it was now evident that it was an absolute siege they were about to undertake, and they were in want of everything necessary for that purpose.

The walls of the little fortress were lofty, and the gates strong—they had neither ladders nor hatchets. There was, however, the possibility of killing Pascal while at the window levelling his musket; but this seemed but a poor chance to men who believed their adversary was invulnerable.

Accordingly, the most prudent manouvre seemed to be to retire out of gunshot and deliberate on their future proceedings; but their retreat was not rapid enough to prevent Pascal Bruno despatching two more messengers of death after them.

Pascal, perceiving that the siege was raised for an instant, went to the opposite window that overlooked the village: the discharge of the muskets had attracted the attention of the first party, so that he had scarcely shown himself at the opening when he was saluted with a shower of bullets; but the same miraculous good luck again preserved him. It seemed like enchantment: while, on his side, every shot he fired told upon the soldiers, and Pascal was made aware of his success by the oaths they uttered.

A similar occurrence happened to this troop as to the other; its ranks were thrown into disorder, but, instead of taking to flight, they stood up close against the walls of the fortress, and by this manouvre they made it impossible for Bruno to fire without thrusting half his body out of the window; and, as the bandit thought it impolitic to expose himself to unnecessary danger, the firing in consequence of this mutual act of prudence ceased for an instant.

"Have we got rid of them?" asked the Maltese; "may we cry Victory!"

"Not yet," observed Bruno, "it is only a suspension of arms; the enemy have, no doubt, gone to the village to procure ladders and hatchets; we shall, no doubt, soon have news of them. But make yourself easy," continued the bandit, filling two glasses; "as we cannot remain quiet with them, we must give them something in return. Ali, go and fetch a barrel of powder.—Here's to your health, captain!"

"What are you going to do with the powder?" asked the Maltese, with an uneasy look.

"Oh! not much; but you shall see!" replied Bruno. Ali entered the room, bearing on his shoulder the barrel of gunpowder.

"That's right," said Bruno; "now take a gimlet and make a hole in the barrel."

Ali obeyed with the passive readiness that was the distinctive mark of his devotion to Bruno.

While this was going on, Pascal tore up a napkin into strips, which he tied together, and rolled them in the powder he took out of a cartridge; he then put this match into the hole Ali had made in the barrel, and closed it with wet powder, which had the effect also of keeping the match in its place. He had scarcely finished his preparations when the sound of a hatchet was heard at the gate.

"Am I a good prophet?" said Bruno, as he rolled the barrel towards the door of the chamber which overlooked a staircase leading to the castle court, and then going back to fetch a piece of lighted fir from the fire.

"Ah!" said the Maltese, "now I begin to understand what you are going to do."

"Father," said Ali, "they are coming from the mountain with ladders."

Bruno ran to the window from which he had fired in the first instance and plainly saw his adversaries, who had procured the scaling implement they so much needed, and, ashamed of their first retreat, were returning to the charge with renewed confidence.

"Are the guns loaded?" asked Bruno.

"Yes, father," replied Ali, handing him a carbine.

Bruno, without looking back, took the gun the boy offered him, slowly brought it to his shoulder, and levelled with more care than he had yet exhibited; he fired, and one of the two men who carried the ladder fell.

Another man took his place, and Bruno took a second musket: the other soldier fell by the side of his comrade.

Two other men succeeded those who were killed and fell in their turn; upon this the scaling party, leaving their ladder, retired a second time, after firing another volley as useless as their previous discharges.

In the meantime, those who were besieging the gate redoubled their blows, and the dogs on their side barked furiously; every moment the blows became more violent and the barking fiercer. At length, one side of the gate was forced in and two or three men entered by the opening; and by the cries of distress they uttered, their comrades judged that they had fallen into the hands of more terrible enemies than they had calculated on; but they could not fire upon the dogs without the risk of killing the men.

After a short time, one party of the besiegers had entered through the door one after the other; the court was soon filled, and then began a combat, like one of those that were exhibited in the ancient circus, between the soldiers and the four monstrous dogs, who fiercely defended the narrow staircase that led to the first floor of the fortress. Suddenly, the door at the top of the staircase opened, and the barrel of powder Bruno had prepared bounded from stair to stair and exploded like a bombshell in the midst of the combatants.

The explosion was terrible; one of the walls fell in ruins, and everything in the court-yard was blown to atoms.

The besiegers were for an instant stupefied; but in the meantime the two troops had united themselves, and presented an effective force of more than 300 men. A deep feeling of shame overwhelmed the multitude when they saw themselves kept in check by a single man.

The leaders took advantage of this feeling to encourage them, and a breach having been made by the fall of the wall, they marched up to it in a body in good order, and having cleared every obstacle, they spread themselves over the whole of the court-yard and were soon before the staircase.

When they reached this spot, there was another moment of hesitation: at length some of them, encouraged by their comrades, began to ascend the stairs, the rest of the party following. The staircase was soon carried; but those who were at the head would soon have felt an inclination to retreat if it had been possible; this, however, was no longer the case—they were obliged, therefore, to attempt the door, which yielded without resistance.

The besiegers, uttering shouts of triumph, ran round the first chamber; but at that instant the door of the second room opened, and the soldiers perceived Bruno seated on a barrel of gunpowder, a pistol in each hand, while the terrified Maltese rushed through the open, doorway crying out, in accents so full of truth and terror as to leave no doubt on the subject:—

"Stand back! stand back!" he cried, "the fortress is mined; if you advance another step we shall all be blown to atoms!"

The door was closed as if by enchantment, and the shouts of victory were changed into cries of terror. The whole body of the besiegers might have been seen precipitating themselves down the narrow staircase that led to the court-yard—some among them leaped through the windows—it seemed as if every man felt the ground tremble beneath his feet, and at the end of five minutes Bruno was again master of his fortress.

As to the Maltese, he took advantage of the opportunity and left the castle.

Pascal, no longer hearing any sound, arose and went to the window. The siege had been converted into a blockade; a guard was placed at every opening, and the men who performed this duty had sheltered themselves from the bandit's fire behind carts and barrels. It was evident that a new plan for carrying on the campaign had been adopted.

"So it seems they intend to starve us out," observed Bruno.

"The dogs!" exclaimed Ali.

"Do not insult the poor beasts who died while defending us, call them men—men!" said Bruno, smiling sarcastically.

"Father!" said Ali.

"Well, my boy," said Bruno, kindly.

"Do you not see?" said Ali.

"What?" asked Bruno.

"That light!"

"Ay, truly," said Bruno; "what can it mean? It cannot be daybreak yet; and, besides, it comes from the north, and not the east."

"The village is on fire!" exclaimed Ali.

"By heavens you are right!" said Bruno.

At that instant loud cries of distress were heard; Bruno rushed to the door and found himself face to face with the Maltese.

"Is that you, captain?" said Pascal.

"Yes, it is I—I myself, don't deceive yourself and take me for another; I come as a friend."

"You are welcome," said Bruno; "but what has taken place?"

"That which has taken place is," said the Maltese, "that, in utter despair at not having taken you, the soldiers set fire to the village, and refuse to assist in extinguishing it unless the villagers will consent to march against you, as they have had enough of it themselves."

"And the peasants?" asked Bruno.

"Have refused," said the Maltese.

"Ay, ay—I knew that beforehand," said Bruno; "they had rather that all their houses should be burned to the ground than touch a hair of my head. Well, captain, go back to those who sent you, and tell them to extinguish the flames."

"What do you mean?" asked the Maltese.

"I will give myself up," said Bruno.

"Give yourself up, father?" cried Ali.

"Yes, but I promised to surrender to one man alone, and I will only give myself up to him. Let them, therefore, as I have said—let them put out the flames, and then send to Messina in search of the man I shall name."

"And who is this man?" asked the Maltese.

"Paolo Tomassi, a brigadier in the gendarmerie," replied Bruno.

"Have you any other request to make?" asked the Maltese.

"One only," replied Bruno, and he spoke to the Maltese

in a whisper.

"I hope you are not asking for my life?" said Ali.

"Have I not told you I should perhaps require your assistance after my death?" said Bruno.

"Pardon me, father," said Ali, "I had forgotten that."

"Away, captain, and do as I have said," said Bruno; "when I see the flames extinguished I shall know my terms are accepted."

"Do you not wish me to be the bearer of the news?" asked the merchant.

"Did I not say you should be my negociator? By-the-by," continued Pascal, "how many houses are burnt?"

"Two when I came away," replied the Maltese.

"There are three hundred and fifteen ounces in this purse, distribute them among the sufferers."

"Adieu!" said the Maltese, shaking Bruno by the hand.

Bruno threw his pistol away, again seated himself on his powder barrel and fell into a deep reverie.

The young Arab extended himself on his tiger's skin, and remained motionless, closing his eyes as if he slept. By degrees the light of the fire expired—Bruno's conditions had been accepted.

At the expiration of about an hour, the door of the room opened, and a man appeared on the threshold, who, perceiving that neither Bruno nor Ali noticed him, gave an affected cough.

Bruno turned round and perceived Paolo Tomassi.

"Ah! is that you, brigadier?" said he, smiling; "it is a

pleasure to send for you—you have not kept us waiting long."

"Why, no," replied the brigadier, "they met me on the road about a quarter of an hour ago as I was bringing up my party, and they said that you wanted to see me."

"It is true," said Bruno; "I wanted to show you that I am a man of my word."

"Zounds, I know that well enough," said the brigadier.

"And as I promised that you should receive the three thousand ducats in question," said Bruno, "I wish to keep my word."

"Perdition!" said the brigadier, with great energy.

"What do you mean, comrade?" said Bruno.

"I mean," said the brigadier, "that I would rather gain three thousand ducats in any other manner—in the lottery, for instance."

"And why so?" asked Bruno.

"Because you are a fine fellow, and men like you are scarce," was the brigadier's reply.

"Bah! what's that to you?" said Bruno; "it will be promotion for you, brigadier."

"I know it," replied Paolo, with a look of despair. "And so you mean to deliver yourself up?"

"I surrender," said Bruno.

"On your honour?" said Paolo.

"On my honour," replied Bruno; "therefore, you may send all those rascals away. I wish to have nothing more to do with them."

Paolo Tomassi went to the window.

"You may all of you retire," he cried; "I will answer for the prisoner: go and report his capture at Messina." The soldiers shouted for joy.

"And now," said Bruno to the brigadier, "we will finish the supper these fools interrupted."

"With all my heart," replied Paolo, "for I have come eight leagues in three hours, and I am dying with hunger and thirst."

"Well," said Bruno, "since you are so well inclined, and as we have but one night to spend in each other's company, let us pass it merrily. Ali, go and fetch the ladies out of the cellar, if they have not been frightened to death."

Ali performed his mission, and the party enjoyed themselves as best they could. In the morning, the brigadier and his prisoner set out for Messina.

Five days after the events we have just related, the Prince of Carini was informed, in the presence of the beautiful Gemma, who had just ended her penance at the Convent of the Visitation, and who had only eight days previously returned to the world, that at length his orders had been executed, and that Pascal Bruno was taken and placed in one of the prisons of Messina.

"In that case, the Prince of Goto will pay the three thousand ducats promised for his capture; see that the brigand is tried and afterwards executed."

"Dear prince," said Gemma, in that gentle voice to whose appeal the count could refuse nothing, "I have always been curious to see this man of whom I have heard so much."

"Your wish shall be gratified, my dear angel; he shall be hanged at Palermo."

CHAPTER X.—THE CHAPELLE ARDENTE.

According to the promise he had made his favourite, the Prince of Carini ordered the condemned man to be sent from Messina to Palermo; and Pascal, under a large escort of gendarmerie, was conveyed to the prison of that city, situated behind the royal palace, and near to the asylum for lunatics.

Towards the evening of the second day, a priest entered his dungeon. Pascal rose when he saw the holy man: but, notwithstanding all the entreaties of the priest, Pascal resolutely refused to confess. The priest continued to exhort him to unburden his guilty mind; but nothing could induce Pascal to perform this last office of religion. And the priest, perceiving he could not overcome his obstinacy, asked him the reason.

"The reason," said Bruno, "is, that I do not wish to commit a sacrilegious act."

"In what manner, my son?" inquired the priest.

"Is not the first condition of a good confession," said Bruno, "not only the acknowledgment of your own sins, but the forgiveness of those of your neighbour?"

"Certainly," said the priest, "there can be no complete confession without that."

"Well," said Bruno, "I have not forgiven; my confession would therefore be imperfect, and I have no inclination to make a bad confession."

"Is it not," said the priest, "more likely that you have such enormous crimes to acknowledge that you fear they will be too great to expect pardon? But comfort yourself, God is merciful; and where there is repentance there is always hope."

"Nevertheless, my father," said Bruno', "if between your absolution and my death, a wicked thought I have not the power to control should—"

"The benefit of your confession would be lost," said the priest.

"It is useless then for me to confess," observed Pascal, "for this wicked thought will rise."

"Cannot you drive it from your mind?" asked the priest.

Pascal smiled.

"It is that thought," said he, "that has kept me alive, father; without that one infernal thought, without that last hope of vengeance, do you think I would have allowed myself to be dragged forward as a disgraceful spectacle to the multitude? No! I would have strangled myself with the chain that binds me. At Messina, I had made up my mind to do so; and I was about carrying my intention into effect when an order came to convey me to Palermo—I thought she would wish to see me die."

"Whom do you mean?" asked the priest.

"She," said Bruno, with bitter emphasis.

"But if you die in this manner," said the priest, "without repenting, heaven, will show you no mercy."

"Father," said Bruno, "she, also, shall die without repenting, for she shall die at the moment she least expects it; she, also, shall die without a priest, and without confession; she, also, shall find, like me, heaven without mercy, and we shall sink to perdition together."

At this instant the gaoler entered.

"Father," he said, "the chapelle ardente is prepared."

"Do you still persist in your refusal to confess, my son?" said the priest.

"I do persist," said Bruno, quietly.

"Then I shall no longer delay the mass for the dead," said the priest, "which I will repeat without pressing you any further; and I trust that, while you listen, the Heavenly Spirit will visit you and inspire you with better thoughts."

"It may be so, father," said Bruno; "but I have no reason to believe it will."

The gens-d'armes entered, unbound Bruno, and led him to the church of St. François de Sales, facing the prison, and at that moment brilliantly illuminated, for, according to custom, he was there to hear the mass for the dead and pass the night in prayer, the execution being fixed for eight o'clock the following morning.

An iron ring was fixed in a pillar in the choir, and Pascal was secured to this ring by means of a chain that went round his body, but which was sufficiently long to enable him to reach the balustrades where the communicants knelt.

The instant mass commenced, the officers of the lunatic asylum brought in a coffin, which they placed in the centre of the church: it contained the remains of an insane person who had died during the day, and the director thought the deceased might as well receive the benefit of the mass that was about to be celebrated for the condemned criminal who was to die.

Besides, there was an economy in this arrangement, both of time and labour for the priest; and as it accommodated all parties, no objection was made.

The sacristan lighted two tapers, one for the head and the other for the foot of the coffin, and the mass began.

Pascal listened attentively during the whole service, and when it was over, the priest went up to him and asked him if he was in a better frame of mind; but the condemned man answered that, notwithstanding the mass to which he had listened,—notwithstanding the prayers with which he had accompanied it, his feelings of hatred and desire for vengeance were still the same.

The priest told him that at seven o'clock on the following morning he would return and ascertain whether a night of solitude and contemplation, passed in a church and in presence of the crucifix, had produced any change in his feelings of vengeance.

Bruno, as may be imagined, when left alone fell into a deep reverie. The whole of the varied transactions of his life passed in review before his eyes, from the days of his earliest infancy to that moment; and in vain he endeavoured to discover in those early days of his life anything that deserved the terrible fate that awaited his youth. He remembered only a filial and sacred obedience towards the kind parents the Lord had given him. He remembered his father's abode——so quiet, so innocent, and happy at one time—which suddenly, became, without his being aware of the cause, full of tears and sorrow. He remembered the day when his father went out, carrying with him a dagger, which on his return was covered with blood. He remembered the night on which the author of his being was arrested as a murderer; when they carried himself, still a child, into a chapelle ardente like that in which he was now confined, where he saw a man chained as he was now.

It seemed to him as if it were some fatal influence, some capricious chance, some victorious superiority of evil over good, through the means of which all the prospects of his devoted and once virtuous family had been so utterly ruined.

And then he even doubted the truth of the promises of happiness which heaven had made to man; he sought through his own distorted vision for the interference of that Providence of which so much was said; and fancying that in this, his extremity, some portion of this eternal secret would perhaps be revealed to him, he bowed his forehead to the earth and prayed—conjured the Deity, with all the fulness of his soul, to interpret to him this terrible enigma—to raise the corner of that mysterious veil which enshrouded his mind— to dispel his doubts and give him confidence here and hopes for hereafter.

His hopes were vain; all was silent excepting that internal voice which still continued to exclaim—"Vengeance! vengeance! vengeance!"

Then he thought the dead were charged to answer him, and that to that end a corpse had been placed near him: so true it is that the most insignificant amongst us all considers his own existence as the centre of the creation, imagines everything is connected with his being, and that his miserable body is the pivot on which the whole universe turns.

He, therefore, slowly raised himself, paler from the struggle he had had with his mind than from any fear of the scaffold, and he turned his eyes towards the corpse—it was that of a female.

Pascal shuddered without knowing why; he endeavoured to trace the features of that woman—(the coffin in Italy is only closed at the instant of interment)—but a corner of the winding-sheet had fallen over the face and concealed it. Suddenly, an instinctive maddening feeling reminded him of Teresa—Teresa, whom he had not seen since the day when he first broke the bonds of God and man—Teresa, who had become mad, and for three years had been confined in the lunatic asylum from whence the coffin and the corpse had been brought—Teresa, his betrothed, with whom, perhaps, he now found himself at the foot of that altar to which he had so long hoped to have conducted her while living, and where, at length, he had been brought by the bitter mockery of fate to rejoin her: she dead—himself about ignominiously to die!

To remain longer in doubt was insupportable; he rushed towards the coffin to satisfy himself, but he was suddenly dragged back by the waist, his chain not being long enough to enable him to reach the corpse, and it held him fast to the pillar; he stretched out his arms towards the coffin, but he was still several feet away from the object he sought to reach.

He then looked round in search of something by means of which he might be able to remove the corner of the veil, but he could discover nothing; he exerted all the power of his lungs in his endeavour to raise the corner of the cloth, but it remained as motionless as marble.

He then turned round with a look of concentrated rage it would be impossible to describe, seized his chain with both hands, and collecting all his strength for the effort, he strove to break it; but the links were too firmly-attached to each other and resisted all his efforts.

The cold perspiration of rage stood on his forehead; he threw himself at the foot of the pillar, placed his head in his hands, and remained motionless and mute as the statue of despair; and when the priest came in the morning he found him still in the same position.

The reverend man approached him quietly and calmly, as became his mission of peace and his office as a minister of reconciliation. He thought that Pascal slept, but when he placed his hand upon his shoulder, the bandit started and raised his head.

"Well, my son," said the priest, "are you prepared for confession? I am ready to absolve you?"

"I will answer you presently, father; but first render me a last service," said Bruno.

"What is it?" said the priest. "Speak!"

"Father," said Bruno, "will you raise the corner of the cloth that hides the features of that woman?"

The priest raised the corner of the winding-sheet. Pascal

had not deceived himself, that woman was Teresa!

He looked upon her for an instant with the deepest sorrow, and then made a sign to the priest to let the linen fall: the priest obeyed him.

"Well, my son," he said, "has the sight of death inspired you with any pious thoughts?"

"Father," said Bruno, "that woman and I were born to be happy and innocent; but she perjured herself, and I became a murderer. She has conducted this woman through madness, and me, through despair, to the tomb into which we are both about to descend to-day. Let heaven pardon her, if it can—I cannot!"

At this instant the guards entered the church to lead Pascal to the scaffold.

CHAPTER XI.—DEATH OF THE BANDIT.

The sky was magnificent, the air pure and transparent; the inhabitants of Palermo awoke as if it had been a holiday— the scholars at the colleges and schools had a holiday, and the whole population seemed to have assembled in the Rue de Toledo, through the whole length of which the condemned man would have to pass to go from the church of Saint François de Sales, where He had passed the night, to the Place de la Marine, where the execution was to take place.

The windows of the houses were filled with women, whose curiosity had roused them from their beds before their usual time, and the nuns of the various convents in Palermo and its environs might be seen moving like shadows behind the gratings of the galleries; while on the flat roofs of the houses throngs of people waved to and fro like a field of grain.

The condemned man was at the gates of the church placed in a cart drawn by mules, and preceded by a number of White Penitents, the first of whom carried the cross and the four last the coffin. The executioner followed on horseback, bearing a red flag; his two assistants on foot, one on each side. Behind these came a body of Black Penitents, who closed the procession, which advanced in the midst of a double rank of militia and regular troops, while, on the outskirts of the crowd, men were running along clothed in long gray dresses, with their heads covered with hoods, having openings for the eyes and mouth, holding in one hand a bell, and in the other a large purse or bag, collecting alms for the deliverance of the soul of the criminal from purgatory.

It was reported also among the crowd that the criminal had refused to confess, and this deviation from the religious ideas entertained by all gave more weight to the rumours which had been spread abroad since the very beginning of his career, of an infernal compact between Bruno and the enemy of mankind. A feeling of terror, therefore, sat upon the curious yet mute population, and no shouts, no cries, not even a murmur, disturbed the dirge of death as it was chanted by the White Penitents at the head of the procession and the Black Penitents in the rear. Behind these last, and as fast as the culprit advanced along the Rue de Toledo, the spectators joined the procession and accompanied it towards the Place de la Marine.

As to Pascal, he was the only one who appeared perfectly calm in the midst of this agitated mass of people, and he looked upon the crowd that surrounded him without humility and without ostentation, like a man who, understanding the duties of individuals towards society in general and the rights of society in respect to individuals, did not repent that he had forgotten the last, nor complained that it avenged the first.

The procession stopped for an instant at the Place des Quatre Cantons, which forms the centre of the city, for so great a crowd were pressing forward from either side of the Rue de Cassero, that the line of troops was broken, and the centre of the road being crowded with people, the Penitents were unable to proceed.

119

Pascal took advantage of this sudden halt to stand up in the cart and look round him, like one about to give a final order or make a last sign; but after a long examination of the crowd, and not seeing that of which he was in search, he fell back on the truss of straw that answered the purpose of a seat, and a cloud spread over his face which seemed to increase until the procession reached the Place de la Marine; then a second stoppage occurred, and Pascal a second time stood up.

At first, he cast a careless glance to the extremity of the place opposite the gibbet, and then his looks ran over the immense crowd that filled the extensive area of the place of execution, and which appeared paved with human heads, with the exception of the terrace of the palace of the Prince de Butera, which was completely deserted. He fixed his eyes upon a rich balcony covered with damask, embroidered with gold, and sheltered from the sun by purple awnings. There, on a species of platform, and surrounded by the most elegant women, and the noblest lords of Palermo, the beautiful Gemma of Castel Nuova was seated, who, anxious to witness the last agony of her enemy, had caused her throne to be raised facing the scaffold.

The looks of Pascal Bruno and the counters met, and seemed to dart flashes of hatred and vengeance: they were still gazing on each other when a strange cry arose among the crowd that surrounded the cart. Pascal started, and turning quickly to the spot from whence the sound came, his features not only resumed their wonted expression of calmness, but a look of joy spread over them.

At this, instant the procession was again about to move on, when Bruno, with a loud voice, exclaimed—

"Stop!"

The word had a magical effect, the whole of the crowd seemed for an instant nailed to the earth, every face was turned to the condemned man, and a thousand eager looks were fixed upon him.

"What is it you want?" said the executioner,

"My confessor," said Pascal.

"The priest is gone," said the executioner; "you sent him away."

"My usual confessor is the monk on my left hand in the crowd," said Bruno. "I did not want the other; but I wish to confess to this man."

The executioner gave a look of impatience and denial; but at the same instant the people, who had heard the request of the condemned man, cried out—

"The confessor! the confessor!"

The executioner was obliged to submit, and the crowd made way for the monk: he was a tall young man, of a swarthy complexion, and seemed as if he were exhausted by the austerities of the cloister; he went up to the cart and climbed into it.

At the same instant Bruno fell on his knees—this was a general signal; on the pavement, in the street, on the balconies at the windows, on the roofs of the houses, every one knelt; all excepting the executioner, who remained on horseback, and his assistants, who stood by his side. At the same instant the Penitents began to chant the prayers for the dying, to conceal by the voices the words of the confession.

"I have been long expecting you," observed Bruno. "I was waiting here for you," replied Ali, for he it was.

"I was afraid they would not keep the promise they made me," said Bruso; "and that you would meet the same fate as myself."

"No," said Ali, "they have kept their promise; I am at liberty."

"Listen then," said Bruno.

"I am attentive," replied Ali.

"There, on my right hand—" Bruno turned in that direction, for his hands were bound, and he had no other means of pointing—"you see a balcony covered with gold embroidery."

"Yes," said Ali.

"On that balcony is a young and beautiful woman, with flowers in her hair—"

"I see her," interrupted Ali; "she is on her knees at prayers like the rest."

"That woman," said Bruno, "is the Countess Gemma, of Castel Nuova."

"Beneath whose window I was waiting when you were wounded in the shoulder?" asked Ali.

"Yes," replied Bruno, "that woman is the cause of all my misfortunes; she forced me to commit my first crime; she has brought me here!"

"Well," said Ali.

"I should not die in peace if I knew that she would survive me happy and honoured," continued Bruno. "You may die in peace," said the youth.

"Thanks, thanks, Ali!" said Bruno, impressively.

"Let me embrace you once more father," said Ali.

"Adieu!" said Bruno.

"Farewell for ever!" said Ali.

The young monk embraced the culprit as a priest is in the habit of doing when he gives absolution to the sinner, and he then alighted from the cart and mingled with the crowd.

"Go on," said Bruno, imperatively; and the procession again obeyed him, as if the speaker had the right to command.

Every one arose; Gemma reseated herself, and the procession moved on towards the scaffold.

When it arrived at the foot of the gibbet, the executioner descended from his horse, mounted the scaffold, climbed up the ladder, and fixed his blood-coloured flag on the cross-piece above, satisfied himself that the cord was well fastened, and threw off his coat that he might have more freedom of action.

Pascal immediately sprang out of the cart, thrust aside with his shoulders the hangmen's men, who wished to assist him, rapidly mounted the scaffold, and placed himself against the ladder which he had to climb backwards. At the same instant, the Penitent who carried the cross placed it in front of the bandit, so that he might see it in its dying moments. The Penitents who carried the coffin seated themselves upon it, and the troops formed themselves into a semicircle round the scaffold, leaving in the centre the two bands of Penitents, the executioner, his assistants, and their victim, Pascal mounted the ladder, refusing all assistance, with the calmness he had hitherto displayed, and as Gemma's balcony was facing him, it was even observed that he cast his eyes in that direction and smiled. At the same instant, the executioner passed the cord round his neck, seized him by the middle of his body, and cast him off the ladder; he then slipped down the cord, and pressed with his whole weight on the shoulders of the culprit, while the assistants, clinging to his legs, pulled at the lower part of his body; but suddenly the rope broke, not being able to bear the weight of four persons, and the whole party, the executioner, his assistants, and their victim, were rolling on the scaffold.

One man arose before the rest—it was Pascal Bruno, whose hands had burst the cords with which they were tied; he stood up in the midst of a general silence, having in his right side a knife the executioner had in his rage at the accident plunged into it the whole length of its blade.

"Wretch!" cried the bandit, addressing the hangman, "you are neither fit for an executioner nor a bandit; you can neither hang nor assassinate."

With these words, he drew out the reeking knife from his right side, and plunging it into his left side near his heart fell dead.

Then there arose a terrific shout and a wild tumult in the crowd, some rushed away from the spot, while others attacked the scaffold.

The body of the condemned man was carried away by the Penitents, and the executioner was nearly torn in pieces by the people.

CHAPTER XII.—CONCLUSION.

The evening after the execution, the Prince of Carini dined with the Archbishop of Montreal, while Gemma, who was not admissible into the society of the prelate, remained at the Villa Carini.

The evening was as delightful as the morning had been. From one of the windows of the room which was hung with blue satin, the room in which the first scene of our history took place, Alicudi might plainly be seen, and behind it, like a vapour floating on the sea, the isles of Filicudi and Salina. The other window overlooked a beautiful park, filled with orange trees and pomegranates; on the right, might be seen Mount Pellegrimo from its base to its very summit, and on the left the view extended as far as Montreal.

The beautiful Countess Gemma, of Castel Nuovo, had remained for some time at this window, her eyes fixed on the ancient residence of the Norman kings, and seeking in every carriage as it came towards Palermo for the equipage of the viceroy. But at length the darkness of the evening increased, and distant objects becoming indistinct, she entered her chamber and rang for her maid, and, fatigued as she had been by the emotions of the day, she retired to rest.

It was late before the prince was able to relieve himself from the kind attentions of his host, and eleven o'clock struck by the cathedral (built by William the Good) before the viceroy's carriage, drawn by four splendid horses, departed at a gallop. Half an hour was sufficient to enable him to reach

Palermo, and in five minutes afterwards, he had cleared the distance between the city and his villa.

The prince hastily proceeded to Gemma's chamber, he attempted to enter the door, but it was fastened on the inside: he then went to the secret door that opened on the other side of the bed, close to the recess in which Gemma reposed. Having opened it softly, that he might not awake the charming sleeper, he stood a moment to gaze upon her in the sweet and beautiful abandonment of repose.

An elaborate lamp, suspended from the ceiling by three strings of pearls, was the only light in the room, and its light was arranged in such a manner as to prevent its dazzling the eyes of the sleeper. The prince, therefore, leaned over the bed that he might see better.

Gemma was lying with her chest almost entirely uncovered, and her boa, rolled round her neck, contrasted beautifully by its dark colour with the whiteness of her skin.

The prince for an instant gazed on the enchanting statue, but its want of animation soon astonished him; he drew closer, and perceived that a strange paleness overspread her features. He bent his ear over her, but could not hear her respiration; he seized her hand, it was cold. Then he placed his arm beneath the form he loved so well, that he might warm it by pressing it to his breast; but he suddenly allowed it again to fall, and uttered a cry of anguish and horror. Gemma's head had fallen from her shoulders and rolled upon the carpet.

The next morning the yataghan of Ali was found beneath

the window!
   THE END.